ROSEMARY'S DOUBLE DELIGHT

Never Give Up

Divine Creek Ranch 4

Heather Rainier

MENAGE EVERLASTING

Siren Publishing, Inc.
www.SirenPublishing.com

A SIREN PUBLISHING BOOK
IMPRINT: Ménage Everlasting

ROSEMARY'S DOUBLE DELIGHT
Copyright © 2011 by Heather Rainier

ISBN-10: 1-61034-502-9
ISBN-13: 978-1-61034-502-6

First Printing: March 2011

Cover design by *Les Byerley*
All art and logo copyright © 2011 by Siren Publishing, Inc.

Tritt, Travis Lyrics. "Anymore." *It's All About to Change.* Warner Bros. © 1991.

ALL RIGHTS RESERVED: This literary work may not be reproduced or transmitted in any form or by any means, including electronic or photographic reproduction, in whole or in part, without express written permission.

All characters and events in this book are fictitious. Any resemblance to actual persons living or dead is strictly coincidental.

Printed in the U.S.A.

PUBLISHER
Siren Publishing, Inc.
www.SirenPublishing.com

DEDICATION

To my husband, thank you for encouraging me to pursue my dream and for your unfailing patience. Brainstorming and doing research with you is so much fun.

To the girls, Tonya, Christi, Jennifer and Lisa, the ones who've stuck by me through all the hard work, made me laugh and talked me off the ledge.

Special thanks to Lisa and Tonya for their special skills.

I owe a debt of gratitude to Diana, Alison, Caroline, Elisa and all the incredibly talented staff at Siren Publishing. It is a pleasure being a Siren author.

ROSEMARY'S DOUBLE DELIGHT

Divine Creek Ranch 4

HEATHER RAINIER
Copyright © 2011

Chapter One

The middle of July…

The humid air hung in the large workshop as Evan stroked loose dust from the smooth oak surface with his hand. The odors of freshly sawn wood and turpentine permeated the shop as the radio played a Travis Tritt song.

"Why don't you call Rosemary tonight?" Wes asked as he turned to the work table, wiping down the framework for the padded bench.

Fucking mind reader.

"Naw. She'd probably rather talk to you, Wes. I don't want to upset her anymore." *Anymore.* Shit, now even Travis Tritt was getting in on the fun, poking at the painful spot in his chest.

Wes continued in a reasonable tone. "Not talking this out is what's upsetting her. She misses you. She wishes things were like they used to be, before…you know."

Evan turned to look his brother in the eye. "Before I fucked everything up. Yeah, I know."

"That's not what I meant. If you call her, she'd be happy to hear from you. It'd be a start anyway."

"We'll see," Evan muttered. The ball was in his court, and he stood there like an idiot watching it bounce away. "She working today?"

"Yeah, she usually takes lunch at eleven thirty," Wes offered helpfully. "I could spare you for a while if you want to take her to lunch."

The lyrics of "Anymore" mocked him as the song came to its final refrain. *"And I'm tired of pretending I don't love you anymore."*

"I'll think about it." Evan looked at his watch. He'd stop at ten o'clock and take a shower. It would be good to talk to her. He missed the old times something fierce.

* * * *

Rosemary chatted with Jack Warner as she folded the shirts he was purchasing into a neat stack on the sales counter at Cheaver's Western Store.

"How are things going with you and those Garner boys?" Jack asked as he handed her his debit card.

"All right, I guess. Wes seems fine, but Evan I don't know about."

"Be patient, sweetheart. He'll come around." Jack smiled at her compassionately. "They're good men, and they deserve a good woman. Plus, they need someone to keep them on their toes. I imagine you're up to that challenge?"

"I hope so. You, Grace, Ethan and Adam give me hope. The wedding plans going all right?"

"Oh, yeah. Are you coming with Wes?"

"Yes. I wouldn't miss it." She handed him his shopping bag.

"Well, hang in there. We'll see you around," Jack said with a wink before strolling off to the front door.

A few minutes later, a woman approached the sales counter and laid several items on it then plopped her over-sized, knock-off handbag down beside them. Rosemary heaved a mental groan, remembering where she'd last seen this oh-so-annoying person.

Several weeks ago at O'Reilley's, the woman had nosily approached Rosemary's friend Grace while she was enjoying dinner with Jack, Adam Davis, and Angel Martinez and had the nerve to question her about the intricate gold necklace she was wearing. The necklace had been a gift from Ethan Grant, and the woman had made some ugly insinuations about Grace accepting such a costly gift from another man when she was engaged to Jack. Rosemary braced herself for whatever venom would spew from the woman's mouth this time.

Elizabeth Owens sighed dramatically and spoke to Rosemary as if she knew her well. "It is such a *shame* that decent, hard-working men around here have the wool pulled over their eyes like that."

Smothering a sigh, Rosemary replied, "I'm sorry?"

Remember it's your mouth that gets you in so much trouble. She's not worth it.

"That *poor* man, Jack Warner. That gold digger he's engaged to is one of *those* women in town. You know, the ones who like *group sex*?" Elizabeth uttered the last two words in a stage whisper meant to be heard. "She's bamboozled him into marrying her. She's stolen three of the most eligible bachelors this town has. Someone ought to run her out of town. We don't need that kind of immorality around here. The bible *clearly* states that—"

Oh, there she goes. Miss Holier-Than-Thou.

Rosemary interrupted her. "We should love our neighbor. You really need to check your facts before you spread any more gossip, Mrs. Owens. If you did, you'd know that Grace is an upstanding member of this community, self-employed, and well thought of by many people. If there's an element of immorality in town, she has been more a victim of it than a perpetrator. Grace loves her men and is devoted to them. I imagine she will make a very happy marriage with Jack, despite what busybodies like you may say about her."

The look on Elizabeth's face was comical. Rosemary grinned when she saw her co-worker Bernadette approach with a smile, having overheard the exchange. Elizabeth's jaws flapped together several times as Rosemary slid the neatly folded stack of merchandise to Bernadette. Rosemary lifted the stack of freshly hung shirts from the sales counter and walked away to place them on the rack.

After finishing with the sale, Bernadette sauntered over and said, "I've never seen Elizabeth Owens struck speechless before. That had to be a first. She's probably going to complain about you, honey."

Rosemary scoffed and said, "Oh, she can bite my lily-white *ass*, Bernadette. What are they gonna do? *Fire* me? That woman and her self-righteous, gossiping friends are an embarrassment to Divine. They can *all* bite my ass." Bernadette first laughed then coughed, looking past Rosemary's shoulder. She quickly excused herself.

"I'd love a bite of that, myself," a deep voice said near her ear. Startled, Rosemary jumped and turned. She knew exactly who it was even before she looked because her body responded to that rugged voice the same way every time. The shirts she was holding swung around her ankles as she turned, catching on her pant legs. Losing her balance, Rosemary fell into Evan's powerful arms. He caught her against his broad chest and steadied her as she juggled the hangers in both hands.

Perfect. Rosemary looked up into Evan's handsome face. His full sensual lips showed the barest hint of a smile. Her body rendered a triple-whammy reaction as she inhaled his clean, soapy scent. Her nipples hardened, and her cheeks became so hot they throbbed, *just* like her clit. She put Pavlov's dogs to shame with her lightning-quick responses to his stimuli.

"Hi." Evan leaned forward to kiss her cheek and she clearly heard him inhale.

Well fine, damn it. I hope he gets hard as a freaking rock. It seems only fair.

"H–Hi. How are you?" she asked. She hoped he could see in her eyes that this was no rhetorical question she was asking.

He gazed at her with turbulent, dark brown eyes, hesitating before finally saying, "Confused, needy, and missing you something fierce. How about you?"

"I—um. The same." She wished the tremor in her breathing would stop. She looked down at the shirts, trying to remember what she'd been doing with them.

"Do you take lunch anytime soon? Could I take you out?"

"Yes, at eleven thirty." Glancing at her watch, she added, "You're right on time. Is Wes around?"

"Naw, just me." He paused for a second before adding, "Is that all right?"

"Of course it is. I'll grab my purse and let the office know I'll be out for a while."

Rosemary hung the new shirts on a rack and walked to the stockroom to check out. She glanced back at Evan and caught him watching her walk away. He had a sexy grin on his face and his cock was definitely taking notice if the big bulge behind his fly was any indication. Good. Knowing he was still affected by her kind of made up for her pebble-hard nipples and sopping wet pussy.

Rosemary stopped inside the stockroom doors for a moment and leaned against the wall, catching her breath. Was he finally ready to talk to her? Could they put the past behind them?

"Carol, I'm leaving for lunch."

Reaching for the ringing telephone, Carol, the office manager and bookkeeper, said, "Your uncle is looking for you, honey."

"I'll get with him later," she said distractedly as she went into her office and retrieved her purse.

Her Uncle Randy had different ideas, though, and caught her just as she was about to walk through the stockroom doors back onto the sales floor.

"Sweetie, you can't be telling the customers off."

Rosemary caught a glimpse of Evan standing at the front of the store talking with someone, before she turned back to her beloved uncle. "Elizabeth Owens is a mean-spirited gossip. I told her exactly what she needed to hear. She was gossiping about Jack, Ethan, and Adam. Did she happen to mention *that* when she came and cried on your shoulder?"

Randy gave her a long-suffering look. "It's bad for business. She talks—"

"We do more business with the Divine Creek Ranch in a week than we do with the whole Owens family in a year. Seems to me like I did the right thing."

Randy nodded and said, "You're correct. But you know that's not how she's going to spin it when she tells everyone how she was mistreated here."

"Oh, she can bite—"

"Your *ass*. I know," Randy said, unable to hide a snicker. Her uncle was her senior by all of five years and had a hard time pulling the age card with her. He gestured with a thumb over his shoulder before crossing his arms on his chest, a big grin on his face. "Did you know Evan Garner is out there?"

Rosemary rolled her eyes. Word always spread fast around Cheaver's Western Store, whether good or bad. "Yes. I'm having lunch with him. I'll be back in an hour…or so."

"Or so?" Randy looked at her, arching a brow. She elbowed him in the ribs as she went past him.

"See you in a bit. Want me to bring you anything to eat?"

"Yeah, if you don't mind. Anita didn't have time to pack me a lunch this morning. Whatever you order is fine." Randy deserved better than "whatever," but Rosemary kept her thoughts to herself.

"'Kay, love you," she called as she stepped through the door. Her uncle treated her better than her own father ever had, but he acted more like an older brother. As indulgent and kind as he was to his wife, he deserved better than the treatment Anita offered.

Evan waited for her, talking to two old-timers sitting on the bench by the door. He smiled as she approached, not hiding his enjoyment at watching her as she walked. When he looked at her like that, she felt self-conscious. She was aware of the way her rounded hips swayed as she walked, aware of her straight posture that pushed her big breasts out, and certainly aware of the throbbing in her clit as he continued to stare at her like a starving man. This was going to be an interesting lunch.

Rosemary held back an appreciative sigh as he opened the door for her, his thick, muscled biceps flexing sexily as he nodded a good-bye to the old men. She wanted to reach out and caress that bulging muscle, but they needed to talk first. She didn't even know where to begin.

"Rudy's?" Evan asked simply as he opened the passenger door for her and helped her climb into his truck. She couldn't help but notice he seemed a little unsure where to begin, as well.

"Yeah, that sounds great. Will you help me remember to pick up lunch for Randy while we're there?"

"Sure. So you've been all right?" he asked, looking out the windshield.

"Mostly, yeah. Wes tells me you're really busy right now."

He seemed grateful she'd broken the ice as he glanced at her and grinned. "Yeah, Jack has us building a whole warehouse full of furniture for Grace."

Rosemary chuckled and said, "They know how to spoil a girl, that's for sure."

Evan put a hand on her knee for a second then drew it back cautiously. "Remember, she doesn't know about all that. She only ordered three pieces, besides the custom bed."

Pavlov's dogs set to barking at his slight touch. "Don't worry. I'll keep the secret. So?"

Evan gulped noisily. "Yeah?"

"Confused?"

He nodded, neither smiling nor frowning.

"Needy? Missing me?" she asked, rubbing her sweaty palms on her jeans.

He kept his eyes on the road and nodded.

Rosemary searched his face, loving every plane and line of it. She liked the soul patch he'd grown beneath his lower lip. She'd liked the way it tickled her jaw when he'd kissed her cheek a few minutes before. Rosemary was glad he hadn't gone for the whole goatee. Evan had such a strong, chiseled jaw that he didn't need to hide it behind facial hair.

Rosemary licked her lips, wishing she could kiss him. Either he'd read her mind or he'd caught her gaze because she heard him groan quietly. He pulled into Rudy's parking lot in one of the spaces in the rear. He sat motionless for a few seconds, looking out the windshield, the engine still running. Evan gripped the steering wheel so hard his knuckles were turning white then abruptly released it and rubbed his hands on his thighs.

He began almost haltingly. "Baby, none of this is your fault. I'm sorry I've been taking it out on you."

"Nope, there is plenty I'm responsible for, Evan. Me and my mouth for starters—"

He held up a hand and cut her off. "That was years ago, baby, and you were right. I *was* a stupid boy. I was stupid for not seeing the big picture. I was a horn dog who couldn't see past his own needs. Marrying a bitch like Rita, there must've been something wrong with my brain."

"Naw. You were just thinking with the *wrong* brain," Rosemary said with a snicker, hoping a little levity would help the mood. Plus, he knew better than to give her an opening like that and not expect her to run with it. "Since we're dredging up the past, you might as well say it." She looked into his eyes and waited.

He paused for a few seconds. "Damn it. Sleeping with my brother? After turning *us* down time after time," he muttered.

"I wanted to wait until after college when we would all be together again. I wanted it to be forever and then you didn't want me anymore—" Rosemary couldn't stop her voice from cracking even after all this time.

He surprised her by not raising his voice and quietly said, "I never stopped wanting you, even after I met Rita."

Anger swelled in her at his words. A fat lot of good telling her that did her now.

"You brought her home and introduced her to everyone, even *me*," she said, her voice trembling again on the last word. "You asked *her* to marry you."

Defensively, he said, "It didn't seem to bother you none—"

"It was *killing* me. You gave me no warning and—"

Evan put his hand on her knee again to stop her. "I'm sorry, Rosemary. This was my fault. Please don't be upset. I shouldn't have said that. Wes told me later that was the first time for both of you."

Taking a calming breath, Rosemary replied, "Yes. Evan, I've only ever wanted the two of you. When he told me you'd divorced Rita, we got our hopes up that you'd come around. What the three of us had was a long shot before, but now…"

"But now, what?"

"I've talked to Jack, Ethan, and Adam, and they're so happy. I'm probably not as sweet and kind as Grace, but I think it could work."

Evan chuckled wryly. "I don't know, baby. Grace can drive a point home with a blunt chisel when she wants to."

Filled with more curiosity, Rosemary asked, "You've talked to her? About other stuff besides the furniture, I mean?"

Evan turned to her and nodded. "Yeah. She came over with the guys one night. I asked her about things and she helped me see it could work. I asked her how she handles it when people criticize her for her choice. You know what she said?"

"What?"

"That Jack, Ethan, and Adam take care of her so well they make it worth it to her, and she said she tries to do the same for them."

Rosemary asked, "Aren't you at least glad it was Wes and not somebody else I slept with?"

Her question seemed to surprise him a little, judging by his expression. He paused for a few seconds before nodding. "Yes. I'd have let him be your first, anyway. You looked like it had been good between you." He shook his head and said, "I wasn't upset about catching you in Wes's bed. I was jealous because I wasn't included. That really says something, doesn't it?"

"If you were making love to me with Wes in the room, he'd care if it was good for the two of us, also. We're a threesome."

"I'm sorry I called you a slut. I never believed that. I said it because I was surprised and hurt, and because I was an ass. Has there been anybody else for you since then?"

She was embarrassed by her immature reaction to his question even as she pulled her fist back and popped him in the arm. She should've known better. His biceps were like granite. "Ow! Ow!" she yelped as she clutched her hand to her chest. "That's none of your damn business!"

No, you ass! There hasn't been anybody else, unless you include my battery-operated boyfriend. She needed to release tension from time to time like any other normal person.

Evan took the hand she clutched to her chest and kissed her knuckles soothingly. "I'm sorry. You're right, that's none of my business. Forget I asked."

Done! Rosemary could picture his smug face if he ever found out she'd been waiting all this time for them.

"So, do we have a clean slate?" he asked, looking hopeful.

Not quite done, she held up an index finger. "Rita?"

"I doubt a bigger, more faithless, lying bitch exists. I have debts I'll be paying on for at least another two years. I haven't spoken to her since our divorce was final in December."

"Do you have any obligation to her?"

"No. I hired a P.I. and made sure. Everything I'm obligated to pay for, I'm paying for, and through the nose. Listen, Rosemary. I'm sorry I threw away what we had together. I promised I'd never leave you then I did exactly that."

"I've missed you very much, Evan. It's in the past. Let's leave it there." She chuckled when she heard Evan's stomach rumble noisily. "Ready to eat?" Rosemary asked, reaching for her purse.

Taking her by surprise, Evan yanked her against his brawny chest as if she were weightless. "There is one little thing." Kissing her with a blistering hot intensity, he cupped the back of her head in his hands as though he'd never let her go. Despite the air-conditioning in the truck cab, the air grew sultry between them as his lips plundered hers passionately and his fingers gently grasped her hair, holding her in place. How his kiss could be so dominating and so tender at the same time amazed her. Desire coursed through her veins, and she was reminded why, even though she had dated, she'd never wanted any other men more than she did this one and his brother. Her out-of-kilter world righted itself in that moment.

Thankfully, the back parking lot was empty except for his truck. She slid her fingertips into his short, neatly trimmed brown hair. She squirmed in his lap and moaned as she tilted into his kiss and pressed her breasts against his chest. He released her to catch his breath, and she giggled and said, "I'd say it's *anything* but little." She wiggled in his lap and pressed against his bulging erection. "Is that for me?" The very thought made her pussy ache for him.

Evan groaned. "Yeah, that and about a thousand others over the years."

Rosemary kissed his lips playfully. "Did the thought of me make you hard?" She shouldn't do this. It wasn't nice to tease him.

"*Very*." He wrapped his arms around her hips and pressed her against his groin. "But it's been worth the wait, to hold you now." He laid his forehead on hers, and she could hear the emotion in his words. "I love you, Rosie Posie."

Her heart lurched, and when she spoke, her voice cracked. "I haven't heard you call me that in years."

"I've loved you forever. Even when you were a hellacious brat. Now you're a beautiful, grown woman. Can you forgive me?"

"Of course."

He nuzzled her jawline, the brush of his soul patch sending shivers skating down her spine again. "I'm sorry for all the wasted time."

"It wasn't all wasted, Evan. We were going to college in different parts of the state for four years. I grew up a lot while I was gone, so I don't believe it was all wasted."

"I'm sorry I made you and Wes wait like this, being so stubborn these last few months. I just didn't think it would work."

She braced herself on his thick, solid shoulders as she climbed off, unsure she wanted to let go. "Wes loves us both very much."

Evan chuckled good-naturedly. "Yeah, but I'm not doing him."

She giggled. "You know what I mean."

He patted her ass before she settled back in the seat. "The only thing we're sharing is you, Rosemary."

She grinned when he shifted in his seat, giving his swelling cock a little more room. He pressed a button on his phone, eyeing her hungrily. Her pussy responded to his gaze with an echoing pulse. "Hey, I'm at Rudy's with Princess Butterbutt. You want me to bring you something?"

He grinned at her gasp when he used the nickname she still despised, and then he laughed as he tried to cover his vulnerable parts when she pinched his arm. "Ow! Yeah, she still *hates* that nickname. Hang on. Here she is." He handed her his phone.

Playfully, Rosemary stuck her tongue out at him and took the phone. "Hello, honey," she said pleasantly.

"Hey, baby. I like the laughter in your voice." Wes sounded happier than she'd heard in a long time. "Did you show him how much you still *love* that nickname?"

Evan had begun calling her Princess Butterbutt in seventh grade to rile her up. Wes had rarely ever used it. He knew better than to make fun of a woman's butt.

"Yes, I showed him all right."

"What time are you done with work today?"

"Five o'clock." Suddenly, it seemed a long way off.

Thoughts of retribution against Evan were forgotten as she detected the hopeful tone in Wes's next statement. "Would you like to come out to the house for a while this evening?"

"Sure, but all we're going to do is talk, all right? No fooling around."

"If you'll come out, I promise we'll be gentleman. I'll hog-tie and gag Evan if I have to."

Rosemary giggled at that image and replied, "Okay. Should I bring anything? Rope?"

Wes chuckled sexily. "No. Just yourself." Her pussy liquefied at the rugged timbre of his voice. "That's all I want. You sound happy."

How she was going to get through this evening with her panties on was anybody's guess.

"That's because I am."

"I'll let you go before I get all sappy. I love you, baby."

A lump formed in her throat. If she stayed on the phone, she was going to do worse than get sappy. She was going to bawl.

"I love you, too, Wes." She ended the call and handed Evan his phone.

"No fooling around, huh?" he said, sounding like someone kicked his puppy.

Ugh! Out of everything he heard, that's *what Evan was asking about?*

Rosemary crossed her arms under her breasts, noting the flare of heat in Evan's eyes. *Suffer, boy! Serves you right. You great, big horn dog!*

"No. We need time to talk and let the dust settle. Being intimate with you, then discovering another slew of problems that we need to deal with would be too much. I need to know we're all on the same page."

Evan gazed at her and caressed her thigh. "When did you get so wise, Rosemary?"

Rosemary was relieved he was being serious about it now. "It's my *heart* we're talking about, Evan."

A little part of her also needed to keep Evan at arm's length until he'd proved she could trust him. Talk was cheap, and she needed time to develop faith in him like she had with Wes. Intimacy would only complicate things, and the last thing she needed was to be thinking with her girlie parts. She already knew what *they* wanted.

* * * *

Junior year of college…

As Rosemary worked through her junior year at Sul Ross University in Alpine, Texas, the need within her for them persisted. One night she called Wes, who was at the University of Texas at Austin, and discovered that all their Christmas break schedules coincided, and they made plans.

Evan wanted her to come back a whole day early and spend the night with them, but she refused. Rosemary knew this time she'd give in to him. To them. She wanted them as much as they wanted her, but she'd be damned if she'd put her goals in jeopardy.

She was meeting them in their favorite spot at Bowie Lake because it might be the only privacy they had this Christmas.

Rosemary searched the waterfront for them as she cleared the bend and...whoa.

Rosemary feasted her eyes. They stood talking at the base of the cypress tree. Evan skipped a rock across the water as he nodded and spoke quietly to his brother. They looked bigger, harder. Wes looked over Evan's shoulder and smiled widely. Rosemary squealed and ran to them, her coat flapping in the breeze. Evan caught her when she gleefully flung herself into his arms. Wrapping her arms and legs around him, she hugged his neck happily. They'd changed since the last time she'd seen them. They were even manlier.

She looked into Wes's glowing green gaze and reached out to him over his brother's shoulders. Evan held her cradled to him as Wes moved to stand beside his brother. She put a hand on both their shoulders, completely unself-conscious of the way Evan held her, until she looked in his eyes. Evan was normally reserved, not quick to reveal much emotion.

His eyes glowed with love. And lust. She became very aware of the hard ridge pressing between her thighs. He was so...big.

Her cheeks grew warm, and Wes chose that moment to break the tension. "Come give me a hug, Rosie Posie." Wes's big jacket opened when he held out his arms to her, and she reached inside it and snuggled against his chest.

Evan stroked her long, unruly hair. She knew he and his brother loved her hair, which was one of the reasons she'd never cut the length off. He'd been giving her that sweet, simple touch since they were in kindergarten together. She pressed her cheek against Wes's muscular chest and turned her head to look at Evan, her heart filled with pure joy.

Her eyes grew misty as she said, "I missed you both so much." She closed her eyes and breathed in the scents of soap and leather. Evan stroked her cheek, standing close to her. It felt so right. She smiled up at Wes as she reached out a hand to draw Evan closer.

They satisfied her need for both of them this way, allowing her to hug them in close proximity to each other.

The wind chose that moment to kick up, and Rosemary shivered at the damp chill in the air.

Wes pulled his coat around her and said, "Let's get you out of the wind, baby."

Wes and Evan led her back to the boathouse near the pier. She ran ahead of them to the deserted structure. Taking a seat on the dock, she let her feet dangle above the water. They entered and sat down on either side of her. She felt bracketed in their body heat, surrounded by her two best friends. Looking from Wes's gentle green eyes to Evan's smoldering brown eyes, she wanted so much.

She wanted them, but she wanted a life with them, too. She wasn't on the pill yet, and she couldn't take the chance of anything derailing her plans for returning to school and finishing well. Rosemary also wanted the whole romantic package. Many people would think it was hokey, but she wanted to wait for their wedding night. She'd been completely faithful to them while she'd been in Alpine.

Perversely, she also wanted to thumb her nose in her father's face. She longed to prove wrong his predictions that she'd wind up with one of them in a common-law marriage with five sniveling brats hanging on her, unable to make ends meet. She wanted to prove to him that she could have her dream.

But she was not immune to their animal magnetism as they gazed at her. She pictured making love to them in this dingy boathouse, their naked bodies entwined, and her body ignited with lust that was tempered only by her lack of experience.

"Could I kiss you?" she asked, looking from one to the other. Wes cleared his throat as he shared a look with Evan over her head. Wes's brows knit together, but before he could say anything, she reached for him. She heard Evan groan and held on to him so that they were all connected as Wes pressed his lips to hers.

He was gentle as he cupped her cheeks and his clean, masculine scent flooded her nostrils. His hands trembled slightly as he held her, and she knew this kiss meant something special to him. He didn't plunge in, because that wasn't like Wes. He finessed her, suckling her lower lip as his fingertips slid to cradle the back of her head. His touch was soothing. When he released her, she felt dazed.

Turning to Evan, Rosemary held on to Wes as Evan drew her snugly to him before he kissed her. That was Evan. His kiss was demanding, but no less loving. He took control of the moment, and she loved that about him, wrapping her other arm around his waist and hanging on tight.

These were not the first kisses she'd shared with them, but they were the first kisses that tempted her to take off her clothes and see what happened. Evan released her, and she saw the need and lust in his eyes and felt it herself. She turned to Wes and kissed him again as they touched her.

Rosemary moaned softly when Wes cupped her breast in his hand and felt the flood of heat and moisture between her legs when Evan's warm hand slid up her thigh. Her heart pounded, and she wondered if Evan would stop before he reached the apex of her thighs. Her clit pulsed in overexcited anticipation.

Her body's explosive response grew as Wes's hand stroked her other thigh. Her earlier resolve was forgotten. Wes slipped off his coat and put it behind her so she wasn't on the bare board. She relaxed against Evan and allowed them to lean her back. They continued to kiss and fondle her. She planted her feet on the dock with her knees bent, which gave them easier access to her thighs. Wes groaned as he kissed her, and Evan nuzzled against her throat and below her ear. His thumb brushed her peaked and throbbing nipple as he cupped her breast, and the tension in her pussy grew to almost unbearable proportions. She felt swollen and hot and in need down there. Wes stroked her abdomen as he released her lips and looked into her eyes.

"You okay, baby?" His protective nature was never far from the surface.

"Yes."

Evan claimed her next kiss, erasing any resolve she had left. As his kiss intensified, she gave in to him, knowing he'd never hurt her, showing her trust in him. The throbbing in her pussy intensified into a hot, burning knot as Evan slid his hand down farther until his fingers pressed between her legs, through the denim of her jeans. Her trembling body responded to the pressure of his fingertips as he stroked her firmly. She felt another flood of moisture and her breath caught in her throat.

Just a little more!

"Feel good, baby?" Evan whispered.

"Yes! Oh, Evan, yes!"

She turned to Wes and saw the warring concern and lust in his eyes. She kissed him to placate his worry for her. Evan stroked upward over her clit and pressed firmly. Rosemary moaned loudly as the tension between her legs wound tight and imploded. The pulses sparking through her cunt seized control of her body so she moved her hips and rubbed her pussy against his hand, hoping for more.

"Evan." Wes's voice was firm, then he kissed her forehead. The pulses faded and she clung to them as she caught her breath. Evan didn't respond to his brother as he pressed heated kisses to her throat. He slid his hand over her abdomen as he ground his hard erection against her thigh. She panted as his fingertips slid beneath the waistband of her jeans. Her bare flesh shuddered at his warm touch, and she gasped in reaction. She wanted his fingers on her so much. But she wanted more. She grasped his forearm to stop him. *What had she just done?*

"Evan," Wes said, more forcefully.

Evan stopped his advance, withdrew his hand, and rested his forehead on her shoulder. A groan escaped him and he whispered, "Baby, need you."

In a steely tone, Wes said, "Now is not the time, Evan. She deserves better than this, and you know it." Evan glared at him and Rosemary was afraid for a moment they might throw fists. But Evan calmed down, and Wes helped her sit up and wrapped his coat around her. She was grateful because she felt a little fuzzy and light-headed. What had just happened? Evan sat up on the edge of the dock and abruptly rose to his feet and walked out.

Rosemary turned to Wes and said, "Wes, I'm sorry." What he must think of her. She'd told them she wanted to wait and then had allowed this rendezvous to go too far. Wes must've stopped his brother because he'd known she'd give in.

"I want you to have your dream. Rosemary. You deserve it. This was a bad idea. We should've met somewhere less secluded."

"I understand if you hate me right now." She was ashamed to realize what she'd done to them. She was a cock tease. It wasn't intentional, but that's what she was.

"Never, Rosemary. Neither does Evan. It's just...painful." Judging by the tremendous bulge at his groin, he must have been in pain. "Let's go find him."

They found Evan down at the cypress tree skipping stones. She was relieved he hadn't left. He looked up when they approached, and she could see the disappointment in his eyes.

He stopped skipping rocks and looked out over the water. "Rosemary, I find you impossible to resist. I'm sorry I pushed you so hard. I didn't mean to frighten you."

She touched his arm. "You didn't frighten me." What could she say to help him understand?

Wes said, "Bro, it's just another year. Let's give Rosemary what she needs. Then she can be all ours."

Evan cast Wes a "fuck you" look, but then gazed into her eyes. "I love you, Rosemary, but you're killing me." He gave her a small smile and kissed the top of her head as she stood at his side and put her arms around him, careful to not press against him.

"I never intended to be a cock tease. I should've behaved myself better."

"I'm the one who should be confessing to bad behavior."

"I'm glad you didn't leave."

"Never gonna leave you, Rosie Posie."

Chapter Two

Rosemary wasn't even out of her car before Wes and Evan were out the front door of their house. She paused, memorizing this moment. It had been a long time since she'd seen Wes's face radiate only joy in her presence. Before, it was always tempered with sadness and longing. Now his green eyes sparkled as he gazed at her.

Prior to that morning, she hadn't seen Evan's dimples in years. Evan was always reserved, much more likely to hide what he was feeling and thinking. What he felt now was plain in his dark eyes as she sauntered slowly to the steps. The glimmer of desire she saw there did her heart a world of good.

Stopping at the foot of the steps, she looked up at them. For the first time in a long damn time, she remembered what it had felt like to be their third, the one that made them complete. They met her on the steps. Wes drew her into his sinewy arms, and kissed her for the first time in forever, it seemed. His kiss was tender but tinged with a bridled fierceness, promising lovemaking that would bring her to utter dependence on him. She'd never hold herself back from him again after that happened.

Tears came to her eyes as she thought of the patience he'd had with her and Evan. Wes's kiss lingered, caressing not just Rosemary's lips but her very soul. Wrapping his arms around her, Wes lifted her to all six feet three inches of him. At a petite five feet three inches, she felt like she was climbing him as she wrapped her arms and legs around him and held on tight. She caressed the short, silky blond strands at the nape of his neck, loving the way his arms felt around her. She sighed contentedly when Evan brushed her long, curly black hair aside and rained wet kisses down her neck and onto her shoulder, his work-roughened hands caressing her back and her arms. Finally, *finally*. Sandwiched between the two of them, something broke loose inside her, and the dam burst on an ocean of tears.

Mutely, Wes carried her into the house. Rosemary wept as Wes sat down and turned her in his lap. She reached for Evan as he sat beside Wes, and he held her so she was lying across Wes's lap, reclining in Evan's arms. They didn't shush her, just let her have her cry. Sniffling and hitching, she looked at them, and the agony she saw in their eyes renewed the flood of tears.

Evan's face crumpled as he cuddled her and shook with his own emotion. He held her like he'd never let her go. "I'm so sorry, Rosemary. So sorry for what I put you through. I can see it all there in your eyes. I can remember what I said, what Rita said, and how much we must've hurt you. I'll regret that forever."

* * * *

Senior year of college…

Wes's Christmas break was turning into a real disaster. It was the senior year of college for all of them. The last time Evan had talked to Wes on the phone, he'd said he had news for them. When she'd talked to Wes, Rosemary had said she thought something was off. Wes had attributed it to the stress of finals. Now they both knew what the news was.

Rosemary turned to Wes and sobbed into his shoulder as soon as they were alone. He'd seen the devastation in her violet eyes, and it damn near killed him. He held Rosemary close and stroked her back as he watched Evan's truck disappear down the curving driveway. Rita, Evan's new girlfriend, sat so far over the middle of the bench seat she was practically in his lap.

Wes had taken an instant dislike to Rita's possessiveness of Evan. She'd made a nasty remark to Rosemary, insinuating that she'd have a catfight on her hands if she thought she'd be getting Evan back now that Rita was around. Evan's surprise visitor had certainly taken Wes by surprise, and her comment had really broadsided Rosemary.

Rita had excused herself to use the restroom, and Evan had turned to them as if nothing were wrong. He had a big, shit-eating grin on his face, and he winked at his brother. Instantly, Wes knew what this was about. Pussy. Rosemary had held out on them all this time, and Evan had gotten tired of waiting.

"She's really something, isn't she?" Evan had asked.

No, in fact, she wasn't. Wes couldn't believe Evan would throw away what he had with Rosemary over someone so trashy. Sure, her jeans were as snug as her top was revealing, but in the looks department, Rita was nothing compared to the angel sitting at his side.

"Yeah, she sure *is*. So are you, asshole," Wes had muttered, putting his arm around Rosemary when she'd started to tremble.

"What? What did I do?"

"What did you do?" Rosemary had whispered. "*You* stupid boy, what did you do? You ruined everything. You told her about the three of us?" Rosemary's fingers had been stiff with tension and cold in Wes's grasp. He'd felt her shaking against him as she'd quietly had her say.

"I'm a senior in college, Rosemary. I have needs."

Wes felt the immediate need to kick his brother's stupid ass. Evan had made a promise to her the year before. Now, with just a few months to go, he was springing this girlfriend on them.

Rosemary had grown still as his insinuation struck home. "Stupid, stupid, stupid. *I wanted to wait for* our wedding night. But now you've got all the free pussy you want. I hope she rips your heart to shreds."

Right on cue, Rita had strutted back into the room. "Well, now that y'all got that little talk out of the way, Evan honey, I want to go dance. I want to meet all your other friends. That is, if you were ever permitted to have any."

Evan had chuckled like he was amused by her sass and said, "Yeah, let's go, baby. Catch you later, Wes. Later, Rosie Posie." Wes had felt the tremor quake through her as Evan had cruelly used their pet name for Rosemary.

Now Wes stood on the back deck with his arms around her while she cried her eyes out, her dreams shattered.

"Honey, his head is straight up his ass right now, and someday he's really going to regret doing this. I can't speak for him, but I love you, and this doesn't change anything. I'm still yours. I always will be, no matter what."

Rosemary hugged him then pressed her fingertips to her forehead. "I know, Wes. I love you, too. I need to sit down," she whispered as he helped her to a chair under the covered patio. "I must be in shock. I feel light-headed."

"I'll get you a glass of water," Wes offered.

"Could I get some aspirin, too? My head hurts," she said, holding her head in her hands.

Wes retrieved what she needed, and she downed the pills with the entire glass of water. He sat down next to her and rubbed her shoulders. Rosemary sat with him in the porch swing as more tears fell. Wes's parents had gone out earlier and were planning to stay overnight at a romantic, new bed and breakfast in Morehead. They weren't expected home until the following night and didn't know yet about Evan's new girlfriend being down for a visit.

The following afternoon, Rosemary called the house and asked Wes if she could come over. Five minutes later, she was standing on his front porch. They sat down in the den and had a heart-to-heart talk. When she asked him to make love to her, right then, Wes could find no strength in his heart to turn her down. He knew it was probably not the smartest thing to do, under the circumstances, but *they were both hurting, and he gave in to temptation. There no longer seemed any reason to wait.*

After taking Rosemary to his bedroom, Wes helped her undress and made love to her the way only a man soul-deep in love with a woman can. What he lacked in skill and experience, he tried to make up for with tenderness and utter adoration. Wes did his best to love her enough for both men.

They had the house to themselves, and Wes took his time with her. He talked to her, whispering love words to her, stoking the fires that had been smoldering for years between them. Drawing on every bit of knowledge he'd acquired on the subject, he'd done his best to prepare her, bringing her to climax after surprising climax, before she ever even saw his cock.

When he finally took her virginity, losing his own in the process, she was so ready for him she came twice more before he finally found his own release. Wes lay there with her, holding her precious little body close, stroking her as she came down from the sensual high. After several long minutes, he carefully withdrew and pulled a sheet over their quickly cooling, sweat-soaked bodies. When he asked if she was all right, she answered him with a kiss as she snuggled closer.

That was the moment Evan chose to barrel through his bedroom door, which Wes had unfortunately forgotten to lock. They'd barely even caught their breath, and the scent of sex was heavy in the air. Evan stood there in silent shock for a few seconds before his dark brows drew together over his eyes.

Wes jerked the sheet to Rosemary's shoulder. "What the fuck! You don't know how to knock?"

"I came to ask if you wanted to shoot some hoops. Looks like you were shooting something else, though. Wow, what a liar you are, Rosie Posie. Thought you said you were waiting for our wedding night. Nothing but a lying slut. Why did I waste all that time when you two have probably been fucking for months, no, years, behind my back?" Evan smirked cruelly before continuing, "Well, now is as

good a time as any to tell you the good news. Rita and I are getting married after graduation. You can go back to fucking now."

Evan turned and slammed the door behind him, but not before Wes heard Rita's irritating laughter from the hallway. Rosemary cringed as Evan also slammed the front door on their way out. At least they hadn't stayed.

Wes held her trembling body in his arms. "I'm so sorry, honey. I should've remembered to lock the door."

Rosemary put her hands over her face and sobbed until she was hoarse. Wes soothed her, but he couldn't find it in his heart to feel bad for making love to her. Sinking into her honeyed heat had been the most amazing, satisfying experience of his life. Rosemary completely captivated him with the way she responded, the way she touched him and loved him. All the waiting had been worth it to share that experience with her. He wondered, as he held her, where they went from there.

Lost in the moment as he and Evan held her, Wes recalled that they'd done the only thing they could do. They'd limped through the Christmas break then returned to school. Wes had finished the final semester with flying colors. Rosemary had done the same thing, graduating with a bachelor's degree in Business Administration. Rosemary didn't attend Evan's wedding, and Wes had attended but refused to be Evan's best man.

Evan had remained in Lubbock with Rita, and Wes had been grateful. Rosemary had devoted herself to the store and her uncle, proving what an asset she'd become to the operation since graduating. Wes had seen Rosemary on a regular basis but it had never felt right after all the time the three of them had spent together. Their history had been as a threesome, no matter how innocent.

Chapter Three

When Rosemary was all cried out, she sat up in Wes's lap. Wes stroked her hot, damp cheek and said, "We're together now, and that's what counts, baby. We have a lot of lost time to make up for, starting now. I know there is plenty to talk about, but let's start with the simple things. Evan is going to grill the steaks for us, and I want to show you the house."

"How do you like your steak?" Evan asked, patting her hip before he rose and went to the kitchen. She watched admiringly as he walked away. Evan caught her ogling him, and she smirked and mimed taking a bite. He lifted the plate the raw steaks were on and waited for her response, eyebrow arched in amusement.

Finally finding her voice, Rosemary replied, "*Oh!* Medium-rare, please."

Rosemary turned to Wes, snuggled up to his muscular chest and reveled in his strength.

"Feel better?" Wes asked as he took the glass of water Evan handed him for her.

She took it from him and said, "Much better."

"That was bottled up from all these years, wasn't it?" Wes asked, caressing her cheek as she nodded and drank the entire glass. Wes took her hand and said, "It's been a while since you've been out to the house, and we've changed some things. Let me show you around."

After she climbed from his lap, he led her to the rooms they used as a home office and library. Wes had always had been an avid reader. Evan was more of a science fiction paperback kind of guy but there were shelves devoted to all their book collections lining every wall in the large room. A sofa, side table, overstuffed recliner, and reading lights filled the center of the room. A large, thick, blue and red area rug dominated the floor, in a swirling paisley pattern.

The office next door contained two large desks with hutches, laptops open at both stations. Pointing at the messy desk, she said, "This is your desk."

Grinning, he asked, "How did you know? Did you see your picture on it?"

She glanced back to the desk and saw the picture he referred to. The framed photograph was taken at Bowie Lake when she was sixteen. Her curls were wild and wind-blown, and she was dressed in a periwinkle blue bikini. All these years, he'd had a picture of her sitting on his desk.

Ignoring the hitch in her chest, she said, "No, I didn't. I saw the Darth Maul PEZ dispenser I gave you years ago. You still have it?"

"It's a collector's item now, but it's precious for other reasons, too," he replied, kissing her. If he kept saying things like that she was going to blubber some more.

Stepping over to Evan's neat and tidy space, Rosemary saw something that nearly did make her bawl again. In freshman art class, their teacher had them experiment with plaster casting, and she'd cast her right hand for him, to use as a paperweight. She'd worried that he might think it was creepy, but Evan had loved it. It sat there, all these years later, atop a stack of orderly manila files. There were fingerprints all over it, like he'd actually used it on a daily basis.

"You and I weren't the only ones holding on, I think," Wes murmured. "Let me show you the rest." Wes led her down the hall and showed her the bathroom, which had been redone, and the third bedroom, which they used for a game room and home theater.

Indicating an empty oak shelving unit with his hand, he said, "I added this especially for you, for your DVD collection."

"Thank you," she murmured, understanding what he was trying to communicate. There was room in their house for her.

"We can have movie parties and entertain back here if you want to. The arcade games actually work."

"You are too much, Wes Garner. This is wonderful," she said, hugging him happily.

"The popcorn machine works, too. The sound quality on the theater system is unbelievable. We need to watch a movie together sometime soon so you can see how great it is. Our friend Sam installed it for us and did a top-notch job. He's wired the rest of the house for theater entertainment as well as sound. He can come back after you get settled and put in whatever you want in the master bed and bath, kitchen, and your office."

"*My* office?" she asked incredulously.

"Sure. Why not? I figured you'd want a room for your own personal use. We can build whatever sort of furniture you'd like in it. You can decorate it however you want."

"Are you asking me to move in?"

"No. Yes. Evan needs to be here for that conversation," Wes said a little lamely.

Rosemary grinned and said, "I'm not living in sin with you, Wes Garner. I haven't held out all this time just to become your live-in girlfriend."

Wes smiled down at her and kissed her, saying, "No one said that was what we wanted, now did they? Patience, princess. Come on." He led her down to the end of the hallway.

He reached inside the darkened room and flipped on the light switch. The walls were painted in the same neutral taupe and the floors were the same medium-toned hardwood as the rest of the house. What stood out about this empty room was the hanging light fixture.

"I know you like Italian blown glass. I found this at an estate auction. I thought you'd like it. Baby, you're gonna catch flies like that," he chuckled, reaching out a finger to close her open jaw.

"Wow."

He grinned triumphantly. "I guess that means you like it?"

"I—I *love* it." Hand-blown colored glass globes held the light bulbs. She saw magenta, light blue, orange, red, electric blue, bright green, yellow, and purple mixed with milky translucent glass and shaped in an artsy, random pattern. "This must've cost a mint, Wes!" Rosemary was impressed that he remembered.

"Trust me. It was worth every cent to see the look on your face. Come on, there's more."

"More?" she asked.

Wes turned to her and gave her that gorgeous smile she loved so much. "Much more."

She followed him to the living room. Dark brown leather furniture was arranged around a coffee table in front of the stone fireplace. There were framed prints of family members on the mantle and on the walls. She was in several of the photos and thought it was nice they'd held onto them. Passing into another hallway on the other side of the house, he led her down to the master bedroom suite.

Rosemary sighed when she entered, feasting her eyes. Wes had redone the walls in an oak plank paneling that matched the flooring. There was another blue and red, patterned rug by the enormous bed, which was drop-dead gorgeous. The bed had tall posters and a framework with a filmy drape over it. The headboard and footboard were decoratively hand-carved with a swirling floral pattern.

Around the room were several other pieces of furniture: a dresser and mirror, a tall chest of drawers, a rocking chair, tall mirror on casters, and a tall lingerie chest. Rosemary crossed the room and pulled one drawer after another. They were all empty. She looked back at Wes, questions in her eyes. He smiled and led her past the large walk-in closet, into the bathroom.

Her jaw fell open again. They had redone the shower and floors with new tile and had put in a humungous bathtub to replace the standard tub that had been in there, if she recalled correctly. Standing in the bathroom, she looked at him then out at the bedroom door, feeling like something was off-kilter somewhere.

"Did you knock out a wall?"

"Sort of. Do you like the tile and countertops?"

"They're beautiful. That big window is wonderful over the tub."

"It's a double window with a privacy shade inside. You press the switch to lower it," he said, indicating the switch on the wall by the window.

"Wonderful. It looks like you renovated the suite, but it hasn't been used. Where are you and Evan sleeping?"

"The bedrooms across the hall. The old master suite and second bedroom."

"What?—Wait! You *added* on a whole new master suite? This is all new since the last time I was here."

Wes nodded. "The master bedroom needed to be bigger anyway. I converted the small bedroom and old master suite into two bigger bedrooms with an adjoining bathroom. When Evan moved back home, he took the second bedroom and helped me finish the addition."

Wes smiled when Evan slid his bulky arms around her waist. He nuzzled the back of her neck with his soul patch, sending pleasant shivers racing over her skin.

Rosemary looked at Wes and asked, "You did all this, for—"

"You, baby," Evan murmured as she turned to him, smiling when she saw his dimples.

"You helped with all this?"

Evan replied, "I convinced myself I was just helping him fix his house the way *he* wanted it. But I knew deep down he was building it for you."

With a light chuckle, Wes said, "Evan spent as much time in here working as I did. We built the furniture earlier this spring."

Approaching the largest bed she'd ever seen, Rosemary said, "It's all gorgeous. That bed is incredible. I really like the carvings."

Wes pointed at Evan.

Rosemary smiled at Evan. "You did the carving?" He nodded sheepishly.

She brushed his warm cheek with her lips, and he murmured, "You can say it, Rosemary. I was a big dummy. I admit it. All I care about now is that you're here and you like it. The steaks are done."

Following them into the kitchen, she ran her hand over the smooth, brown and black marble countertops. She opened one cabinet after another, looking for plates and glasses.

"Well, one thing hasn't changed," she said, laughing.

"What?" Wes asked.

"The last time I visited, you'd just finished the house and hadn't gotten settled yet. That was two years ago, and these kitchen cabinets are *still* a freaking organizational disaster! An egg beater in the cabinet with the plates. Why?"

Evan laughed as she squatted down, delving into a cabinet to see what else she might find.

Wes replied, "I can't honestly say, honey. I'm a guy?"

From the interior of the cabinet, her voice sounded muffled as she spoke. "Smarty-pants. Well, now I know what my first priority is. Look at all these nice organizers you installed. This kitchen is going to be awesome after I get done with it!"

Patting her rear, Wes said, "Let's find what we need for now and sit down and eat."

Rosemary brought three plates to the table then filled glasses with ice for tea. "What you've done around here is really something—it's beautiful but…"

"What, Rosemary?" Evan asked, casting his gaze away from her. Tension returned to his body language. She'd known him long enough to know he was bracing himself.

Wes looked at him and turned to Rosemary. "What is it, baby?"

"I'm not going to be your live-in girlfriend. Best you know that up front. I can hear my dad over the phone right now." His unreasoning opinion didn't mean shit to her, but she was determined to have her dream, which didn't include a live-in arrangement. She could just imagine how he'd gloat. Then, of course, there was her mom. A totally different type of trouble, that woman would bend over backward to further piss her dad off. Vengeful harpy.

Wes and Evan both relaxed and chuckled a little. Wes spoke first, "We didn't expect you to move in with us, Rosemary. But if I'm investing in a house, it should be the way that we would *eventually* want it, right? I thought it was a good idea for you to know who the extra spaces were for but not because we want you to move in tomorrow. Shoot, crazy as things are right now, we wouldn't have time to move you in, even if you were willing."

"Whew! That's a relief," Rosemary said, feeling even more relieved as the guarded look left Evan's face and his dimples returned. She wasn't the only one who needed time to trust again.

"Besides, we haven't even proposed yet," Evan bravely added.

Rosemary stopped chewing her steak and went quiet and still. Wes rolled his eyes and looked like he wanted to plant his booted foot in Evan's ass.

"Smooth, Evan."

Rosemary quietly returned to chewing, her eyes bobbing back and forth between Wes and Evan, waiting to see what more would be said.

She took it as a good sign when Evan grinned and his eyes twinkled. "That wasn't exactly how that was supposed to come out. What I meant, Rosemary, is that you need time and we need time, to sort of…court, I guess." Color swept over Evan's cheeks as he continued. "We need to give this a chance to feel normal, being together again. What's the matter? Were you waiting for us to start fighting?" Evan slid a heated palm over her forearm, raising chills that ran up her arm and down her back.

Rosemary swallowed finally and grinned. "I was waiting for the smackdown."

Wes laughed and replied, "Really? We haven't had a fist fight in years, have we, Evan?"

Appreciating the levity, Rosemary looked from one to the other and said, "Look at it from my perspective. We're going to have issues that need to be worked out. We were inseparable for years. We know each other better than some couples do before getting married, but in some ways, we're strangers. Evan, you and I especially have a lot of time to make up for."

Wes rubbed her shoulder. "And that's where we are right now. There's no rush to make drastic changes in anyone's status. We can move forward together, now. But we want you to know, with all that said, that pretty bedroom in there is already yours. You're welcome to stay here with us anytime you want to. Bring a toothbrush and a bathrobe to keep here, or not. Start rearranging the kitchen tomorrow, or next year. Your options are all open as far as I'm concerned. I want to take one day at a time."

Rosemary was cheered by that notion, but said, "I feel like there are all these threads of our lives together that were shredded and scattered, and now I've got to pick them up and start weaving them back together again."

"I know, baby," Evan murmured. "I feel that way, too, and it's kind of…"

"Overwhelming?" she offered. He met her eyes when she said it, and he nodded. She looked at Wes with misty eyes and smiled. "Remember? This is the moment I was hoping for. A chance to start over."

Wes gripped her hand. "Yeah. Here we are."

Chapter Four

Late July, a few weeks later...

Wes groaned as his cock sat up and begged. He walked behind Rosemary as she flounced angrily up the back steps in front of him, completely oblivious to how her cute, little bubble butt swayed with each step. Under other circumstances, he would've had his hands all over her right now. Wes could hear her cursing under her breath between sobs as she opened the sliding glass door and stomped inside. She stood in the sunshine streaming in through the door, her creamy skin glowing with coconut-scented tanning oil and the hint of a tan.

"Rosemary, I'm sure Evan didn't mean to get so pissed off. You know that. He was upset that the customers were ogling you, is all," Wes interjected over her sputtering anger. Turning her so she faced him, he could feel Rosemary shaking as he held on to her upper arms. Her face was tear-stained and flushed rosy with anger.

"Well, then why did he yell at *me*? On the one hand he tells me—*you both* tell me—I can come and go as I please, do what I want while I'm here. He knew I'd be here. I *told* him I was going to be sunbathing."

Wes hated trying to second-guess what Evan was thinking and detested being in the middle, *again*. "Evan thought you'd be in the backyard, behind the privacy fence. It was probably the reason he took David and Steve around to the sidewalk on the west side of the house, so you wouldn't be disturbed. His heart was in the right place, Rosemary." He wasn't looking forward to the coming confrontation, and he hoped Evan cooled down before he returned to the house.

"His heart *wasn't* in the right place when he embarrassed me in front of those men. Call me crazy, Wes, but yelling at your girlfriend does not make a good impression on customers. That much I *do* know," she said sassily as she wiped her oiled hand across her cheek and let loose a hitching sob. She looked up at him with those brimming, angelic eyes, and he felt that goofy damned flutter he'd gotten in his chest when she looked at him like that ever since he was six years old.

But facts *were* facts. Wes put his hands on his hips and gestured to the cherry-red string bikini she was wearing. Three little triangles and a bit of string was *all* that the bikini consisted of. His dick twitched in voracious approval. "Rosemary, *look* at what you're wearing. Hell, *I* don't want anyone else seeing you dressed that way. I'm not happy David and Steve saw you practically naked, *either*."

Rosemary gestured to the thickly treed yard. "But it's the afternoon. There's too much shade in the yard. Where else *would* I be? Evan could've called out for me to see where I was. I *never* would've been out there if I'd known people were coming over. He startled me so badly I jumped before I remembered my top was untied. I don't think they saw much before I got it adjusted. I'm sure it wasn't the first time they ever saw a half-naked woman."

Maybe not, but it was his half-naked woman they saw. "That's *not* helping your situation, baby."

Rosemary turned back to him and asked, "Would he really spank me, Wes? He was awfully angry, and I understand why. I can even sympathize with you both. I wouldn't want any of my girlfriends to see *your* goodies, either. But *so help me*, if he ever puts me over his knee, I'll neuter him," she said sharply, sparks in her eyes. "He has to sleep sometime. He'd *better* be joking because that spanking would be the last you'd see of my happy ass."

Wes wished Evan hadn't said anything about spanking her. That was a conversation to have when they were all rational, not in the heat of the moment like this. Ethan Grant had been clear with them about that after Evan asked him. He'd evidently forgotten Ethan's suggestion that they introduce erotic spanking to her first so she wouldn't be afraid of it. The purpose of a chastisement spanking was to get her attention and motivate her to have a care for her own safety, not to actually hurt her. Now here she stood, thinking Evan intended to hurt her to teach her who was boss.

"I don't think he really meant he would actually—" Now it was time for Wes to sputter. *Fuck a fricking duck, where is Evan? He'd better get his ass in here before she gets wound up any tighter.*

"Don't speak for me, Wes," Evan said quietly as he entered the front door and closed it firmly.

* * * *

Evan closed his eyes, trying to gather his thoughts as the image of the skimpy G-string she was clad in danced through his mind. Rosemary stood grim-faced, her arms crossed under her generous, round breasts, pushing them up even higher, so they were barely covered by the twin triangles of her tiny, red bikini top. She might as well have been standing in front of him naked, the perfect silhouette of her torso and her supple thighs like a siren song to his lust-soaked brain. His hands clenched at the thought of stroking her perfectly curved ass, and his eager cock twitched in agreement.

He wished he'd kept his damn mouth shut. Then he might be doing something a little more pleasant than arguing with the little spitfire. Evan opened his eyes as Rosemary turned to face him. His heart lurched as Rosemary lifted her chin, and her lip trembled. Her tear-stained cheeks were red, and he could see more tears brimming in her eyes. He was not proud of himself at all.

Praying for wisdom, Evan said, "Wes, I need to talk to Rosemary alone. You reckon you could give us a few minutes?" Wes gave him a warning glance, and Evan nodded at him. He had no intention of spanking Rosemary now. That, in itself, told him he never should've brought the issue up in the heat of the moment.

Evan and Wes had talked recently about circumstances like this at Jack, Ethan, and Adam's urging. Jack, Ethan, and Adam literally had the whole of their adulthoods to work out how they'd handle problems like this. It was a damn good thing the men had made the time to share their wisdom for dealing with problems and settling priorities. Adding to the mix that Evan and Rosemary's personalities tended to be volatile at times, Wes and Evan knew they were going to need all the wisdom they could get.

Wes nodded quietly, went in the office, and closed the door. They'd recently agreed between the two of them that in an argument between Evan and Rosemary, Wes had to make himself scarce. Rosemary had the tendency to go to Wes for sympathy, which unfortunately, only made things worse. Reconciliation between the two who were arguing had to occur before she could have any contact with the other brother.

Rosemary stood there looking like she wanted to smack him in the face, but the tears in her eyes told him how much he'd hurt her feelings and embarrassed her. Evan wanted to be careful here and not screw things up more than he already had.

He held out his hand. Hesitantly, she took it, and he led her down the hall to his bedroom. For the sake of his sanity, he reached in a drawer and handed her a white T-shirt. She drew it over her head, after surreptitiously pressing her nose to it, breathing in his scent. That little gesture on her part went a long way toward easing his nerves. Sitting down beside her on the end of the bed, Evan lifted her small hand in his grasp. He played with her fingers, drawing his fingers down the length of each one, before lifting her coconut-scented palm to his lips.

There was a point in their relationship where this would've been about the power struggle, pure and simple. Now, he could plainly see the important thing was coming to some kind of understanding and reconciling with Rosemary.

"I'm sorry, Rosemary. We told you this was your home away from home. I can't very well get mad at you when you sunbathe where the sun is best. I had no idea *that's* what you'd be wearing. I'm really sorry I startled you and made you jump up because it's my fault you were exposed. I saw David's and Steve's faces, and it made me angry that other men saw you like that. I shouldn't have yelled at you. The truth is I love that tiny little bikini on you." Just not when other men were around.

He must've done okay apologizing because she pressed her forehead against his shoulder and replied, "I'm sorry, too, Evan. I should've asked if there were going to be people coming over before wearing this. Next time I'll stay in the backyard. I'm sorry I yelled back at you. They probably thought I was a real harpy."

Evan grinned and said, "Harpy? No. Firecracker? Yes, probably." Truthfully, he loved that she was a little spitfire. It kept life interesting.

Rosemary crossed her arms under her breasts again, so the red material was visible through the white cotton. "About that spanking you threatened me with?" she asked, looking at him pointedly.

Cautiously, Evan turned so he faced her on the bed. "I can imagine how you feel about that. Making threats like that was not cool at all, I know, but hear me out, okay?"

She scoffed lightly. "*This* should be interesting."

Evan didn't reply in kind to her comment because she had a right to question his intentions. "From time to time, we have customers who want to see the shop, see samples of what we can do. A lot of our business is done on the internet but not all of it. Customers come from San Antonio and Austin, sometimes from Mexico. We've always welcomed visitors, but that doesn't mean we do background checks on them. What if someone showed up and you were here alone and exposed like that? What if the visitor mistakenly assumed that if you were willing to expose that much flesh you might also be available for some uninvited attention? We'd never forgive ourselves if something happened to you."

"I can see your point of view, Evan. But what does this have to do with spanking me?"

Evan noted that while she was still determined to get to the issue that concerned her most, she didn't seem like she was ready to walk out over it. Maybe she was more curious than concerned.

Forging ahead, Evan asked, "Would you agree, now that you see it from a different perspective, that seeing to your safety should be a higher priority than finding a sunbathing spot with premium sunshine?"

"Certainly, but—"

"I'm getting there, baby. It was a mistake on my part to threaten a spanking in front of the others, and I apologize for doing that to you. But now that you know you're safer in the yard, if you ever endangered your safety like that again, I'd spank your ass bright pink."

Her full, pink lips popped open in surprise. "You would *not*," she whispered, her cheeks flaming with color. Evan noted that she didn't immediately hop up and flounce out of his room. She sat there quietly, evidently thinking about what he'd said. Evan also noticed that she squirmed a bit where she sat. Was the thought of a spanking turning her on? He loved her enough that he'd risk offending her to keep her safe, but it hadn't occurred to him when this discussion began that she might be intrigued by the idea.

"I would, baby, I promise. Your well-being and safety have become my number one priority. If you endanger either, I'd spank you to get your attention and teach you to be more careful. If I didn't care about you, *adore* you, I wouldn't care whether you laid out buck-ass nekkid on the front lawn. We'll clear out some of the trees in the backyard to allow more sunlight for you if that's what you want. Hell, we'll put in a pool for you if it's something you'd like back there, but I won't tolerate you putting yourself in harm's way."

Uncertainly, she replied, "I'm used to taking care of myself and being on my own. I'm sure I'm going to do things you view as 'endangering' myself from time to time."

Evan sensed that this was not the moment to equivocate. She needed the truth, and she needed to know where he drew the line. "Well, you'd better start considering some of those things, Rosemary. I'm not going to go looking for reasons to spank you. I don't want you afraid of chastisement when we're together. But you shouldn't push it, either." His last words drew her gaze to his, and he saw…something there before she looked away. Interesting. He could almost hear the gears turning in her head.

Rosemary gave what he said some thought then nodded. "Okay, but what if I *misbehave* and don't realize it's a spanking offense?" She gave him the innocent-eyed angel look, but he saw the way her full upper lip curled slightly as she suppressed a smile.

Evan chuckled and leaned into her space a little. "Well, misbehavior is something totally different. If you were a naughty girl and needed a spanking, I might have to pull down your panties and spank your little heinie over my knee until you promised to be a *good girl*."

She gasped and squealed when he reached for her and began tickling her on his bed. Rosemary was very ticklish, so it didn't take long for her to beg him to stop.

"So am I forgiven?" he asked, poised over her on his now messy bed.

Beautiful and breathless, she nodded. "If you'll forgive me for yelling at you like that. I'm really embarrassed they saw my chee-chees." She giggled when he rolled his eyes at her use of his juvenile term for breasts while they were growing up.

Evan gathered the hem of the T-shirt he'd given her and tugged it up to reveal the breasts in question and growled, making her giggle again. "Damn, woman, but these are some fine breasts you have here. I can't believe I was so hardheaded for so long. I could've been feasting on this bounty all these years."

Rosemary scoffed playfully, but there was a tender quality to her words. "I *know*. But I saved them for you, didn't I?"

"Yes, you did, now when are you going to break down and let us make love to you? I'm available at a moment's notice." He pressed his solid erection against her hip while kissing her cleavage. He understood she had her reasons for wanting to wait to have sex, and he couldn't rightly blame her. The reason was mostly his fault. It had been a few weeks since she'd come back into their lives as part of their threesome, but she hadn't spent the night yet.

Evan supposed Rosemary was waiting for the other shoe to fall. Waiting for the first confrontation, the first argument, to see how things went. He thought they'd handled it like adults, apologizing and compromising. Evan knew he and Rosemary were both a little hotheaded, and he was not so foolish that he believed because they'd handled this little setback well that it would all be peachy-keen from there on out. Life for them was going to be a series of confrontations and, hopefully, reconciliations until they figured out ways to avoid all but the most important conflicts. Rosemary needed assurance that what they had wasn't going to flat-line at the first sign of difficulty.

As for her little crack about misbehavior, Evan had a feeling he and Wes were going to see plenty of it, judging by her reaction and her words. While he'd been tickling her on the bed, he'd caught the scent of her arousal as she wiggled and squirmed beneath him. Her fragrance made his mouth water for a taste, but he was going to do like Jack had suggested and put her in the driver's seat. As much as his cock hated him for it, if she knew she was in control of the timeframe and didn't feel pressured, she'd come to them sooner rather than later. His cock thought that was a stupid-ass plan and wanted *in*, now.

"Soon, big boy. I don't want to go there until I'm ready."

Evan nodded in understanding. He knew first hand, once you flipped that switch, it was damn near impossible to unflip it. Even though it had infuriated him during that fateful Christmas break, the sight of them in bed together, glowing with satiation, had been riveting. It made his cock twitch and his balls draw up now, thinking how much he'd missed her and the three of them together, and for how long.

If he hadn't had his head up his ass, or more accurately, if he hadn't been thinking with his dick, they probably would've been long-settled by now. The thought made him sad and renewed his desire to earn her trust.

"Don't be upset, Evan. I just need a little more time."

He nodded and smiled, encouraged that any trace of her earlier upset was gone.

"I want to do one thing for you, now that we've worked things out," Evan began carefully.

"What's that?"

"Give you a safe word."

"A safe word? Why?"

"Because you seemed interested in the idea of erotic spanking. Wes and I won't do that unless you've been provided a safe word."

"Oh, okay. I trust you. I don't see why it's necessary."

"You need to have a way of calling an immediate halt to whatever kind of play we're involved in, especially spanking. The safe word would apply to any kind of spanking. Not just play spanking."

"You mean if you were punishing me, I could—"

"Call an immediate halt to it. It needs to be a word that you don't normally use in conversation."

She paused and thought for a few seconds. "Boomerang."

"Boomerang it is. If we're ever doing something together and you want it to stop immediately, say 'boomerang' and it stops."

Rosemary rolled her eyes at him and smiled. "All right. But I think it's unnecessary."

"People wiser than us said it should be non-negotiable that you have a safe word."

"Who?"

"Ethan Grant and Grace Warner."

"Oh."

"Why don't we go find Wes and let him know everything is fine?" Evan said, rising from the bed and offering her his hand.

They found Wes still in the office with the door closed, working at his desk. He looked up from his laptop cautiously. "So? Are we all okay?" Evan felt guilty at the guarded look on Wes's face.

Rosemary smiled at Evan when he released her hand and directed her to his brother, sensing that was what she was waiting for from him. She reached for Wes, and Evan watched his brother relax as his arms slid around her hips to pull her to him.

"Yes, honey. We're all okay. I'll be more careful in the future, and I won't be sunbathing anywhere besides inside the privacy fence. Evan said he would clear some of the post oaks out of the yard so it gets more sunshine back there."

Wes pressed his nose to her belly and inhaled. "Sure, baby. We can do that. We probably should've taken care of that already. They get pretty thick around here."

Evan smiled as Rosemary stroked her fingertips through his brother's hair, reassuring him with her touch that all was well. "You don't have to clear them all. I love oak trees, even post oaks. Just clear enough so I can sunbathe."

Evan crossed his arms over his chest and leaned against the door jamb. "I told her we'd also see about putting a pool in back there. She liked that idea."

Rosemary turned her face to gaze at him and said, "You spoil me. Skinny-dipping is sure going to be fun!" She laughed out loud when they rolled their eyes and groaned.

Chapter Five

Rosemary was willing to admit it was morbid curiosity, balanced with a huge portion of mistrust, that had her sneaking out to the workshop in the afternoon of the following day. Not mistrust in her men, but in the woman who belonged to the disembodied voice she'd just heard. Though she was pretty sure she didn't know the owner of that voice, she definitely recognized the sexy, dulcet tone as the woman walked past the house on the other side of the privacy fence from Rosemary. That was the sound of a woman on the prowl.

Rosemary was currently up to her elbows in landscaping mix, fortifying the soil in the empty flowerbeds that lined the back veranda before planting Mexican heather. Wes had mentioned to her earlier that morning that they were expecting a visit from a supplier in San Antonio. Evidently, the account representative was a woman who'd visited with Rosemary's men on more than one occasion, judging by her familiar tone.

Rosemary frowned and took notice when the woman dropped a not-so-thinly-veiled innuendo after Evan mentioned that Wes was tied up in the workshop. Rosemary heard a seductive laugh and a comment concerning what she'd do if she had either of them tied up in the shop. The Mexican heather could wait a few minutes.

For Evan's part, it seemed that he ignored the comment. Rosemary slipped to the fence and peeked through the slats. She watched as the woman stroked Evan's arm as they walked along talking. Evan's hands were down in his pockets, and he did not look at the woman but sidled a few inches farther away as he walked with her to the shop. Rosemary smiled at his subtle reaction.

The woman didn't seem to notice and kept on talking. If this was a business contact, Rosemary wouldn't want them to brush her off too brusquely unless she was more overt once she got in the shop, behind closed doors. Rosemary dealt with her fair share of friendly suppliers and account representatives working at Cheaver's. They were a mixed lot. Some were super friendly and helpful professionals, and then there were some for whom the job was a chance to socialize and network, sometimes taking the contact further than necessary.

Evan and the woman disappeared through the wide double doors of the workshop a moment before Rosemary quietly raised the latch on the side gate of the privacy fence and slipped through. She convinced herself she had a right to know how the men handled someone like this because she was sure this was not the only female account rep they had to deal with. Stopping beneath one of the opened windows on the side of the shop, she leaned against the exterior wall and listened to the woman make her pitch.

Rosemary had only gotten a small glimpse of her through the fence, but it was enough to know that the woman was a statuesque blonde, dressed in a red pencil skirt that stopped at the knees and a snug, white knit top and tall, metallic heels. She was everything that Rosemary was not, dressed as she was in her gray yoga pants, thin, pink tank top, and wild ponytail.

The woman, whose name turned out to be Davina, covered all the pleasantries with Wes as he finished varnishing a table top. Wes and Evan discussed what they'd need from her employer and took care of business before Davina gradually dropped into a more flirtatious mode of conversation. It was obvious she found both men attractive and, in irritation, Rosemary missed some of what Davina said because she dropped her voice down to a lower, sexier pitch.

"Are you coming to the trade show and convention on the Riverwalk this fall?" Davina asked, her voice sounding as if she were moving around the shop.

Rosemary detected the barest hint of irritation in Wes's voice. It sounded like he was still working on the tabletop. "I don't know, Davina. It depends on how busy we are."

Still moving, Davina murmured, "I'll be in the convention center at our booth. You should stop by. We could go clubbing on the Riverwalk afterward. I booked a nice, big suite at the Aurora Suites downtown. Maybe the three of us could get together and have some fun?" she added in a clear invitation.

Rosemary's heart raced, and her ears perked up, wondering what their response would be to that. She didn't have to wait long.

"It's nice of you to offer, Davina, but Evan and I are involved in a committed relationship."

Rosemary almost snickered Bart Simpson-style, wondering if Wes was playing back in his head what he'd just said to her. Proving she wasn't one of the sharper crayons in the box, Davina paused then said, "Wait a minute. I thought you were related."

Rosemary rolled her eyes. This woman obviously didn't know her men all that well.

When Wes replied, she could hear the smile in his voice, "We are, Davina. We're brothers, but we're involved in a relationship. We have a woman in our lives we're very much in love with. If we went to the trade show and convention, we'd probably be spending every spare minute of it with her." Rosemary's heart flew at the happy, free tone he used explaining to Davina. "But we appreciate your offer."

"Speak for yourself, big boy," Rosemary mouthed silently to herself. She didn't appreciate the offer one damn bit, but she sure did appreciate his words. They were turning down an easy lay for her.

"You mean you're sharing her? As in a *ménage*?" Davina didn't sound terribly put off by that notion. Rosemary wasn't sure it was a good idea to share that information with her, but it did make both her men inaccessible to Davina.

Evan responded, "Yes."

"Ooh. Lucky girl," Davina said suggestively.

"We're the lucky ones." Evan's tone held the barest hint of a defensive edge.

Sounding unconcerned, Davina continued, "She sounds like fun. Maybe you'd like to—"

Rosemary couldn't believe her ears as she fought a full body shudder. *Double fucking eww!*

Wes quickly cut Davina off before all the words were out of her mouth. "*No*. Not happening, but thanks for the…thought." Rosemary cringed and blessed Wes for cutting her off when he did. Now the thought of Rosemary sharing her men with another woman for a weekend was lodged in her brain, making her feel a little nauseous. Rosemary did not consider herself to be prudish at all, but a girl had to draw the line somewhere.

Davina's tone remained light. "Oh well, you never know…I guess I'll see myself out, guys. I'll make sure you get what you need. Appreciate the business and good luck with your…girlfriend. I mean it. She really is a lucky girl."

"Thanks, Davina."

Evan's succinct response said it all for Rosemary. Both her men were prone to use endearments with women they were friendly with. They were waiting for Davina to leave, not encouraging any further banter with her. One of the double doors swung open then shut, and Rosemary heard a growl then a metallic clicking sound.

"I'm calling Papillion," Wes muttered. "Rosemary would be pissed as hell if she knew the extent of that conversation. I doubt Ed would be too happy, either, to know that his account representatives acted like that toward customers out in the field. I know we're pretty casual around here, but damn, Davina's over the top."

"If that's who you're calling, ask if they can start sending Cruz out to visit us from now on," Evan said with a chuckle. "Rosemary wouldn't object to a middle-aged, pot-bellied, balding guy, I don't think."

Wes laughed before saying, "Hi, Carol, how're you? That's good. Could I talk to Ed?"

Rosemary stepped away from the window quietly and made her way back to the gate and slipped inside, smiling. That was a revealing exchange. She felt guilty for spying but was grateful they'd be willing to make a change like that to keep her happy and avoid trouble. It was more confirmation that things would work out between them. She was becoming more hopeful every day.

* * * *

Late August...

Rosemary daydreamed as she went around the store gathering the things she needed for the fall displays. There were four large alcoves used for seasonal displays around the store, one up high on each wall. After Randy was finished lifting and securing the heavy saddles and other items into the tack department display, he brought Rosemary the ladder and reminded her to be careful.

Removing wrappings from the boots, she smiled to herself because tonight was a special night. Rosemary had a special outfit planned for their dinner date and had stopped off at their house to put something sexy in her walk-in closet to change into later that night.

The three of them had been back together for almost two months. That feeling Rosemary had for a while, worrying about the next big blowup, had eased considerably.

They seemed to be handling differences of opinion, even arguments, well. Rosemary noticed the day of the string bikini incident, and on other occasions since then, that she could no longer go to Wes for sympathy when she got upset at Evan. She'd made a habit of doing that over the years, and she saw now that doing so set Wes and Evan at odds.

Luckily for Rosemary, she had Grace to talk to. Grace gave good advice and provided a listening ear but didn't always give her sympathy, helping her see that sometimes she created her own difficulties.

Once Rosemary had climbed into the alcove, Bernadette and another employee handed the boots up to her until they were all in the loft with her. This display contained a small bale of hay, which Randy had lifted into it earlier for her. She scattered some of the layers from the bale, and strewed loose hay around for affect then arranged each pair of boots. She held on carefully and climbed out onto the ladder, sitting on the top step to put the finishing touches on the display.

Reaching into the display to straighten a boot, Rosemary was startled when an angry voice from fifteen feet below bellowed up at her, "Get your ass down from there before you lose your balance and fall!"

Evan startled her so much she knocked the snakeskin boot from the display. She heard several gasps from customers and co-workers alike as she looked down at Wes and Evan. She stood and turned to face the ladder and clutched the sides, breaking out in a cold sweat as the adrenaline rushed through her system.

"Come on down carefully, baby," Wes said, raising his palms to her and speaking in a voice meant to calm her. "Good going, Evan."

She made her way down the ladder until her feet were back on the sales floor.

Evan's eyebrows were drawn over brown eyes so dark they could've been black. "Rosemary, what the hell were you thinking climbing into and out of that display? Do you know how high that is? What were you doing sitting on the top step?" Evan asked in a low, incensed tone.

Rosemary bristled at the tone he was taking with her in front of others. "I'm always very careful." She hated that she sounded like she was making excuses. This was part of her job, after all.

Evan invaded her space with a growl. His big, calloused hand grabbed hold of one of her ass cheeks and squeezed hard. "If I see you up that ladder, putting yourself in danger like that again, or hear about it, I'm turning this little ass bright pink, you understand? You were warned about stuff like this."

Rosemary's cheeks blossomed with heat when she heard a feminine gasp from the dressing room a few feet away. Yep, her day was now complete. Pride reared its ugly head.

Rosemary shoved against his broad chest. "You don't get to tell me what I can or cannot do, you big, dumb jerk. No wonder you're divorced, if this is how you treat women."

Stupid, stupid, stupid...

Rosemary knew her mistake the second the words flew out of her mouth. Instead of apologizing, she kept talking, like that was a good idea.

"I've been doing this job a long time, and I don't need you to be my keeper. I've been patient with your bossiness, up until now. If I'd fallen from that ladder, it'd be *your* fault for scaring the hell out of me. I'm suddenly not hungry. I think you need to leave," she ground out, cancelling their lunch date.

Damn it, why did she let her pride and her mouth sabotage her like this? Why did she always let Evan's hot temper spark her own?

Never one to back down from a confrontation, Evan leaned in to her, his eyes glittering angrily. "You're the same spoiled-rotten little brat you always were, Rosemary Piper. *Just like Rita*, you have to have your own way in everything. You haven't changed one damned bit," he snapped at her then turned on his heel and stalked from the store.

Rosemary bit her lip at his harsh words, knowing she'd pushed him too far. She looked into Wes's eyes and saw his frustration at being caught in the middle, before he turned and walked away, too.

Bernadette sidled up to her, and led Rosemary from the sales floor back to her office. She collapsed into her chair and proceeded to bawl her eyes out. In a small town like Divine, this would be all over the gossip grapevine and probably already was.

Chapter Six

Evan Garner fished his keys from the pocket of his jeans as he pushed open the front door of The Dancing Pony and stepped out into the lingering late August heat. The sun had set hours before, but heat still emanated from the concrete sidewalk. Climbing in the four-door truck, he pulled around to the front entrance then dropped his head to the steering wheel.

Somehow, he had to make this right with Rosemary. Why could he not leave well enough alone? Things were going so well, and he could tell Rosemary was gradually beginning to drop her defenses with them. He'd had a feeling tonight might've been the night she stayed with them and allowed them to make love to her. Then he'd gone and screwed it up, going all alpha male on her, *again*. He prayed for wisdom and the right words to say.

As he prayed, the past came to mind. A past that was pervaded with Rosemary Piper, the same way the typical fall heat still permeated the air inside the truck. He had few memories growing up that were not inhabited by the fierce, little ebony-haired beauty. Wes was hopefully speaking with her right now and convincing her to come home with them. Memories came rushing back.

* * * *

"Mama says I'm a real good cooker," Rosemary chirped as she used a stick to mix the blades of green grass Evan had brought her into the mud pie then sprinkled gravel on top.

"What are you gonna cook for us, then?" Evan asked as he scooped up another handful of mud for her so her hands wouldn't get so dirty. She took it in both of her chubby, little six-year-old hands and placed it on top.

"How about beef stew?" his brother Wes said, filling the bucket from the water hose for her.

"No, how about chili? I want some chili!" Evan said.

"No, beef stew!" Wes crowed, laughing as he sprayed Evan's bare feet with the water hose.

"No, chili! And cornbread!" Evan hollered back, standing in front of Rosemary so she wouldn't get wet or splashed with mud.

"No beef—" Wes was about to say more when Rosemary interrupted.

She was hunkered down, resting her cheeks in the palms of her hands as she looked at them and grinned. "I have a better idea. When you can't decide what you want for me to cook for you, that's when you take me out to eat. That's how it's going to be when we're married," she said with a shrug, reaching over to sprinkle more sand on top of her mud pie.

"Which one of us you gonna marry?" Evan asked. He wanted Rosemary to say him. He'd take her out to eat all the time if that's what she wanted, and he'd eat whatever she cooked.

"Both of you, silly!" she said with a giggle as she reached in the bucket that Wes put beside her with one of her mom's measuring spoons and sprinkled water on the mud pie.

The boys snickered, and Evan said, "You can't marry both of us, Rosie Posie."

"Sure I can."

Wes gave her a double handful of mud and replied, "How come you want to marry both of us?"

"'Cause I could never choose between the two of you. I'm in love with both of you!" she said dramatically and giggled.

Like two red-blooded six- and seven-year-old American boys will do, they croaked and made gagging sounds in the back of their throats, which made her cackle while she poured more water on the pie until it overflowed onto the grass.

"Yeah? And how are we supposed to share you if you're our wife?"

"Just like how you do now. I'll cook for you and do your laundry and maybe even kiss you if you're sweet to me!" She grinned as they did more croaking and gagging. "And you'll take me out to eat all the time, and let me go shopping and put gas in my car for me. That's how it works, and that's what I want," Rosemary said like she was stating the obvious.

Wes looked over at his six-year-old brother and said, "Well, I guess we could both marry you, then. Deal?"

"Deal!" Evan replied.

Rosemary giggled and said, "Deal!"

Wes kissed her on one cheek and Evan kissed her on the other, and they all three ran to the swing set in her backyard.

* * * *

Rosemary's heart lurched as Wes approached her and Mr. Webster on the dance floor. When Wes tapped Ace on the shoulder, he immediately stopped waltzing with her and turned to Wes, eyebrow raised.

"May I cut in, sir?" Wes asked politely, obviously not looking for a fight. Ace turned to Rosemary, waiting for her acceptance or refusal. His hold on her was solicitous, not territorial, but she could tell by the look in his eyes that he noted her tension.

Her eyes welled with tears as she said, "No." She felt tired. Tired from work, certainly, but mostly tired from the emotional overload earlier in the day.

Wes implored her, "Rosemary, please, let me apologize. I'm so sorry." Her tears overflowed at the pain in his beseeching gaze. He had done nothing to apologize for. Evan should be the one begging for forgiveness.

"No." Her voice quavered, and her chin trembled. "How much longer am I supposed to suffer?" Her cheeks tingled as she recalled she'd dealt out her fair share of suffering to others today. There was a small voice whispering to her that she had little right to complain.

"The lady told you no. It sounds like she means it," Ace added quietly, evidently aware all eyes in the vicinity were on them.

Wes gazed levelly at Ace. "Sir, I don't mean any harm. I'd do anything to make this woman happy again." Looking at his handsome face, Rosemary knew he was telling the truth, at least for his part. His dumbass brother was another story. She still wanted to punch him in the face for comparing her to Rita. Evan couldn't possibly know how much that had hurt her.

Rosemary turned to Ace and smiled up at him. "Thank you, Ace. I'll come back to the table soon."

Ace patted her lower back and leaned in. "I'll back off, but I'm not leaving you alone with him. If he gives you trouble, I'll be nearby watching," he murmured, gesturing to the table their group had been sitting at.

"Oh, it's not like that, Ace. I've known him a long time. He'd never hurt me," she reassured him.

A tear picked that moment to overflow, and Ace whispered, "Tell your eyes that, darlin'." He stepped away from her, looking at Wes with warning in his eyes.

Rosemary stepped up to Wes on the edge of the dance floor. "You want to make me happy, Wes? You tell that fool of a brother of yours to bite my ass!" she muttered angrily. The memory of his hand coming down on her ass and squeezing hard would've been a happy memory under different circumstances. He was seriously messing up her spanking fantasies by going there.

"He was worried about you, baby."

"If that's how Evan shows me that he cares, I'm going to have to take out extra disability insurance. I was perfectly fine doing my job, and he had no business interfering. I climb that ladder all the time. It's a part of what I do at the store. He can't go sneaking up on me like that."

Wes didn't sound angry at her, but she could tell he was becoming frustrated. "You scared the hell out of him."

"I? I scared the hell out of him? You were there, Wes. I was perfectly safe. He embarrassed me in front of the whole store. I'll never live this afternoon down. And you're defending him, aren't you? Tell you what, both of you can bite my ass!" She spun on her high cowgirl boot heel and sashayed away from him.

Rosemary heard Wes mutter, "Damn it." He pulled her back to him, causing her to collide with his chest, the impact clouding her senses with his clean, slightly spicy scent. Her lips pressed together in a firm, thin line to keep them from trembling. She was angry, but she still wanted him, if the moist ache between her legs was a good indicator. She glanced up and was held captive by the pleading in his green eyes.

"Baby, all three of us have been in love since kindergarten. I've loved you practically my whole life." Her heart wrenched at his earnest tone and her tears finally overflowed. "Evan never meant to embarrass you. Yeah, his mouth got away from him, but let him explain and apologize. Things were looking so good. Don't let it all go down the drain over a misunderstanding, baby. Please come home with us for a little while so we can talk it out. It's killing us seeing you dancing with another man."

That was what set all this off? Rosemary wanted to scoff but didn't think Wes would appreciate it. Back at the table, Kathleen had mentioned to Ace that Rosemary loved to waltz when a good waltz number played. Ace was being a gentleman by asking her to dance.

"It was just a dance. It didn't mean anything," she whispered. It weighed on her heart that jealousy had prompted them to action rather than guilt. As usual, Wes was the peacekeeper.

Wes stroked her upper arms, still holding her to him. "Come with me so we can talk. Then I'll take you home if that's what you want."

"One of these days, we're gonna break each other's hearts, and it's not going to be fixable with a little talk."

Wes nodded in understanding, evidently sensing she was near capitulation. "You and I are doing our best to not let that happen. Talk to him, and maybe you'll be able to understand why Evan did what he did."

"He insulted me and threatened to spank me in front of the whole store, Wes. There is no way to misinterpret that."

"Evan just wants you to be safe, baby."

"He wants to control me—"

Wes shook his head. "Baby, he *loves* you. His temper got the better of him, and he knows he made a mistake. Please come with me. Everyone is watching us now." Rosemary looked around and saw that he was right. From the security of Eli Wolf's arms, Rachel Lopez even watched, sympathy in her eyes. Ooh! If Rachel knew what these men were putting her through, she'd—

Rachel would tell her in no uncertain terms to get over it and look at the big picture, damn it. She'd probably also tell Rosemary to grow up. That was the cool thing about Rachel. Over the years, Rosemary could rely on her to be honest with her, even when it hurt.

Rosemary's shoulders slumped, knowing for better or worse they needed to clear the air about a lot more than whether or not she climbed a wooden ladder at work. This might be the other shoe dropping, and that thought made her dread their talk.

Looking up at Wes, Rosemary nodded. "Let me get my purse and say goodnight. I'll be right back." As she walked away, she heard Wes sigh with relief. Knowing how hardheaded both she and Evan could be, Rosemary didn't allow herself to feel as hopeful as Wes sounded. She said a quick goodnight to her girlfriends and to Grace, reassuring them she was all right.

Why couldn't things be simpler for the three of them? When he wasn't being an ass, Rosemary loved Evan as deeply as she loved Wes, but these power struggles were getting old, as were Evan's issues with Rita. He'd actually compared Rosemary to Rita, and she could not abide that. A spoiled-rotten brat she might have been in years past, but she'd grown up, and she didn't deserve what he'd said to her. The big bully.

The air definitely needed to be cleared, but it might not end the way Wes and she hoped it would. Guilt reared its ugly old head again because she knew she wasn't innocent of causing them pain, either. There was plenty of blame to share. History had proven on several occasions that little Rosemary Piper was often no better at controlling her mouth or her temper than Evan Garner was. She returned to Wes and took the hand he offered her as he led her out the door.

* * * *

The first day of sixth grade…

The first day of sixth grade had been a terrifying experience for Rosemary. She and her classmates were used to Divine Elementary School with a total student population of 110 children.

Divine junior high school students were bussed to campuses located halfway between Divine and Morehead. It was so much to process, how large the school was compared to the little classroom her twenty classmates had shared for six years. Add to that the necessity of moving from one room to another between classes for eight different periods and a locker with a combination she had to remember. To say she suffered from culture shock was putting it mildly.

The real horror came during PE when she discovered she'd have to change into a scratchy PE uniform while surrounded by 100 other adolescent girls. They'd have to use the communal showers afterward and then dry off with a towel the size of a postage stamp. Her towel was too small to cover her little, round body for the short walk back to her gym locker.

By the time the last bell had rung, Rosemary was completely numb. She felt lonely as she found her locker and gathered her books. Rosemary couldn't wait to see Wes and Evan. She'd missed them all day. She didn't have any classes with them, and the one glimpse she'd gotten of Evan during the day had made her want to cry because he hadn't seen her. She rested her forehead against the cold metal frame of the locker and closed her eyes.

She felt familiar, callused hands on her arms as she stood there. As she turned to them a commotion broke out in the next row of lockers. Evan squatted down to get a look underneath.

"It's two girls fighting," Evan said. "That's the second fight I've seen today."

"Come on, Rosemary. We don't want to miss the bus on our first day of school. Got all your stuff?" Wes asked as he gently tugged on her arm.

After she nodded, Evan slipped her backpack off her shoulders and slung it over his own, evidently unconcerned that it was pink canvas.

Rosemary followed them to the schoolyard, where all the kids waited for their school buses to arrive. Though they only lived half an hour from Morehead, the bus ride would take well over an hour by the time she was dropped off in front of her house. Following them mutely, Rosemary noticed Wes kept looking down at her, the concern plain on his face. Wes hugged her, quietly asking her if she was all right. She felt Evan's fingers slide through her wild, curly hair. For the first time all day, she felt her world return to order.

Rosemary had been close with Wes and Evan since they were itty-bitty, and they'd always looked after her like this. It was a comforting gesture and one that brought tears to her eyes with its easy familiarity, after a day that had been utterly foreign. Her chin quivered, and she pressed her lips together tightly.

"Your day suck as bad as mine, Rosie Posie?" Evan asked, fingering one of her unruly locks. Rosemary nodded and ignoring the crowd around them, focused on Evan gratefully as he continued. "Coach popped everyone who ran late coming out of the showers with a wet towel. I've got a big, red welt on my butt. I can still feel it stinging." The quiver in her chin stopped as he grinned sheepishly and rubbed the aforementioned butt cheek. She knew he was making light of his pain to help her feel better.

"You have to take showers, too?" she asked, her heart beginning to lighten somewhat.

Wes chuckled. "Yeah, nobody warned us about that, did they?"

"No! I was in a room with a gazillion other nekkid girls," she muttered, laughing when the boys gagged and made puking sounds. "At least we didn't get popped with a wet towel."

Wes slung an arm around her and hugged her again.

It was at that precise moment they drew the notice of three sixth-grade girls and a boy waiting in the line next to theirs. Rosemary recognized the boy from her science class, where he was seated next to her. She'd taken an instant dislike to him that morning when he'd flicked one of her tight, curly locks with his freshly sharpened pencil, poking her with it and marking her new white shirt. He'd asked her if she'd stuck her finger in an electrical socket. Hardy-har-har, like she'd never heard that one before. She'd given him an evil look and ignored him.

Now his jeering voice crowed over the rest of the chaotic noise on the schoolyard. "Hey, look! Curly Girlie has a boyfriend. No wait! She has two boyfriends! Are you gonna kiss 'em?" he asked in a singsong voice.

Rosemary looked on in shock as the three little girls standing with him began laughing, and pointed at her. They took up the boy's chant, "Kiss! Kiss! Kiss!"

Turning to Wes and Evan, Rosemary saw their features turn from shock to stone-cold anger. She looked back to the other group, and now the whole line was laughing and pointing at them.

It was hard enough to survive this first day. Add to that her desperate need to fit in and find her place amongst these students, and poor Rosemary made a life-altering mistake.

At the top of her lungs, Rosemary screamed loud enough for everyone to hear, "They aren't my boyfriends! They aren't my boyfriends! I don't like them at all!" Her fellow classmates from Divine Elementary School turned, round-eyed, and gaped at her. They all knew Rosemary, Wes, and Evan were seldom apart.

Bus number 11 pulled to a stop in front of their line of kids. Wes and Evan lifted their backpacks from the ground and turned from her. Evan glanced back at her as the kids in the other line continued to giggle and point at her. His eyes were filled with tears of betrayal. Wes's shoulders were slumped, but he didn't look back at her, just stumbled forward in the line. She opened her mouth to speak, even touched him, but he shrugged her hand away.

Rosemary looked at the boy, and he stuck his tongue out at her triumphantly. She turned away in defeat. She already knew she wasn't going to be friends with him or those bratty girls, but now she'd lost her two best friends, and for nothing. Once on the bus, Wes and Evan made their way to the back seat. Unused to riding a school bus, her instinct was to follow them, but she knew she couldn't do that now.

She was looking for an open spot when her friend Rachel Lopez beckoned her over. In tearful relief, Rosemary collapsed on the seat.

"Wow! Rosemary, you're just as dumb as a brick, aren't you? Are you okay?" Rachel asked, as always balancing wit with compassion. Thankfully, the insult wrapped in sympathy kept her from crying.

"I dunno," she whispered. Rachel patted her shoulder and left her in peace. Rachel made sure the other kids left Rosemary alone on the ride home.

At home, Rosemary flopped on her bed and came to the realization that she needed to apologize. She had to make this right. Right now. Otherwise, seven long, lonely years lay stretched before her. After walking the short distance to their house, she asked Mrs. Garner if she could talk to Wes and Evan.

Mrs. Garner said of course she could but then kindly asked, "Rosemary, how was your first day?" Rosemary could've sworn Mrs. Garner was a mind reader sometimes.

Rosemary looked at the woman and finally cratered. Mrs. Garner held her as she sobbed and told the whole mortifying story. Compassionately, Mrs. Garner patted her back and smoothed her hair then shared a similar experience from her own life.

"Honey, I guarantee you're going to survive sixth grade. It doesn't feel like it right now, but you will. This does explain why Wes and Evan were so quiet when they got off the school bus earlier. They're in the backyard. Why don't you go work all this out? Take these with you." She handed Rosemary a paper plate with chocolate chip cookies Mrs. Garner had baked for them.

Carrying the plate of cookies, Rosemary stepped out onto the back deck of the Garner house. Wes and Evan were occupied with their soccer ball. At first, she thought they didn't notice her there, but after a while, it became apparent they were waiting for her to make the first move.

She enticed them with the snack first. "Hey! I've got cookies."

The boys ran over to where she sat on the deck petting their cat. They each picked up a cookie and stood there munching on them, looking at her guardedly.

"I came to apologize. What I said was so wrong, and I don't even know why I did it. *I* hate *that boy*. He was mean to me earlier today, and when he got all those other kids laughing at me, I just...lost my mind." All her pent up tears streamed down her face, and her voice shook uncontrollably as she spoke. "I feel like my heart is breaking, and I wish I could take those words back." She paused at the looks on their faces. Now they were furious. Did she say something wrong? Did they not believe her?

"He was mean to you? What did he do?" Evan asked, his grubby hands curling into tight fists.

Wes grasped her hand in his. "Yeah, what did he do?"

Relief coursed through her. "He flicked my curls with a sharpened pencil and put a mark on my shirt," she replied, pointing at the gray mark on her shoulder.

"That rat bastard!" Wes muttered. "He could've hurt you."

"His pencil was sharp, and it poked me through my shirt."

Evan snarled and said, "Son of a—"

Rosemary put her finger to her lips. "Evan, you want your mama to hear you talking like that? She'll wash your mouth out with soap again. Let me get this all out, okay?" Rosemary needed to tell them everything. Otherwise, she might never get the guts again. "When they started laughing at me, I wanted to make them shut up. We laugh about gross boy-girl stuff all the time, but I really do love you both, like always. I'd be your girlfriend if you wanted me to."

She finished with a pounding heart, braced for the gagging and puking sounds to begin. Both boys just stood and stared at her. Her heart started pounding, and she felt an icy chill race up her spine.

Wes spoke first while Evan looked on silently. "What are you going to do when that boy teases you tomorrow when he sees you with us?"

Rosemary grinned at him and said, "I'm not going to do anything but watch my boyfriends beat the crap out of him." Wes laughed out loud, and she gladly went to him and hugged him hard, so relieved they still were her friends. She turned to Evan, who was still quiet, although he looked like he'd enjoyed the mental image of punching that jerk's face in. "Evan, can you forgive me? Please?"

Evan looked her in the eye and she caught a glimpse of the pain she'd seen earlier. She tugged on his shirt sleeve. He finally hugged her and said, "You know, we'd have kicked his butt right then if you hadn't said what you did. I wish you wouldn't have been ashamed of us."

She'd really hurt him, and she hated the way that felt. Speaking from her heart, she said, "I'm so ashamed of myself. I'm sorry I hurt you. You're my best friends, and I'm lost without you."

Stepping back, Evan looked at her, stuffing his hands in his pockets, and said, "Of course I forgive you, Rosie Posie. I can't stay mad at you." He grinned and added, "But you're gonna have to get a handle on that mouth if you still want us to marry you."

When he said that, they all fell laughing on the ground making puking, gagging noises.

Chapter Seven

Wes held the door for Rosemary as they left The Dancing Pony. Evan's big pickup truck was pulled over to the curb, waiting for them. Her palms went damp, and she frowned, not ready to face him yet.

As she stopped on the sidewalk, Wes asked, "Is your car here?"

Rosemary shook her head. "No, I rode with Kathleen and Bernadette."

"Come on, baby. It'll be fine," Wes encouraged her quietly. He opened the truck door and helped her climb in. There was country music playing in the background, and the dome-light came on, revealing Evan's stoic countenance.

That was something Rosemary always had difficulty with. Evan was hard to read because he tended to hide his feelings, unless they happened to explode like today. Wes's emotions showed in his eyes, but Evan had a mask he could throw on in a heartbeat. He wore it now.

Wes pulled the door closed, and they headed toward the house. The darkened interior of the truck was quiet except for the radio. Wes held her hand on the seat between them, stroking her palm soothingly with his fingertips. They rode in silence.

Rosemary's nerves were stretched to their limit by the time they pulled up to the house. Evan shut off the engine, climbed out, and held out his hand to help her from the truck. Normally, she'd have climbed out on the passenger side with Wes, but Evan was making the effort, so she wordlessly went to him. Maybe that would communicate something to him, encourage him to doff the mask he was still wearing, but he simply helped her then released her to walk over to the porch on her own. Her shoulders slumped a little, and she braced herself for whatever would come from this conversation.

The house was cool compared to the high temperature outside, even though the hour was late. Wes turned lights on in the kitchen and living room. Evan sat down at the kitchen table, and she joined him. She sat with her clammy, icy hands clenched together in her lap once Wes joined them. He took one of her hands in his.

"Baby, your hands are like ice," Wes murmured and rubbed it between his warm, callused ones. She still had no idea what to say that would make a difference. She was utterly stumped and looked at Evan and Wes, her eyes brimming with tears. It shouldn't be this hard.

Chin wobbling, she finally spoke. "Maybe it would be best, if we…let each other go. Left each other alone. We keep hurting each other, Evan, and we hurt Wes in the process. My *mouth* keeps getting me in trouble with you. It—it shouldn't be this ha–*ard*." Along with the sob that escaped, a dull ache began in her chest. "I guess I can't make you happy. I upset you and hurt you, and you *hurt* me, and maybe we're not good for—for each other. I can't live like this." She paused her babbling, unable to catch her breath through the hitching sobs in her chest, and looked into Evan's eyes in time to catch the crumbling of his mask.

* * * *

Evan was ready for their little firecracker to come out fighting. It's what he'd expected the moment she'd climbed in the truck. Her silence on the drive home was unusual. She was always one to take the bull by the horns. What he wasn't prepared for was the forlorn hopelessness in her eyes and the defeat in her voice.

"*No, no, baby. Please* don't say that." Evan didn't care how he looked as hot tears overflowed, and his shoulders slumped in defeat as his inner resolve left him. He reached across the table for her other hand and placed it against his cheek and kissed it. "*Please* don't leave me. You were *right*. It's no wonder I'm divorced. I don't deserve you if I can't keep my emotions in check better. When I saw you on that ladder, I didn't stop myself when I should've. I know better than to yell at you and embarrass you like that. There has to be a way we can make this work, Rosemary." He went to her and knelt by her chair, looking into her eyes with desperate hope. "You're the only woman that can make me feel alive. I love you. Please forgive me." *Oh god, please don't leave me.*

"We say we love each other, and then we hurt each other and we hurt Wes, which is even worse because he's always in the middle."

Evan looked at Wes and saw him wipe his eyes. Wes knew what this meant. If they broke up now, it included Wes, and it was going to be for good this time. Evan knew Wes wanted Rosie even if Evan wasn't in the picture, but she'd made it clear she couldn't be happy without both of them. If that had been a possibility, they would've gotten together years before. For her, it was all or nothing, and Evan wanted to give her what she wanted. He wanted it for Wes, too. Wes had earned her trust, and he deserved her more than Evan did.

"Please, baby, please don't think that breaking up is the answer. I love you so much. I adore you," Wes whispered, his voice cracking. "*We* love you and have wanted you *so long*. Forgive Evan, for all our sakes. I'll keep him in line myself. I'll shove my fist down his throat if I have to. We just got you back. We need you and want you in our lives so much."

Evan swiped his tears away with the back of his hand and said, "Rosemary, I'll let Wes beat the crap out of me, rather than hurting your feelings again. I only want to love you and take care of you." Judging by the doubtful look on Rosemary's face, they were not making much headway, and Evan couldn't blame her. He'd promised to hold his temper in check and not yell at her or embarrass her after the sunbathing incident. His track record was not impressive so far.

Verifying his thoughts, she asked, "How are you going to make these changes? It's obvious they aren't going to happen because we wish them to."

"What if I talked to Ethan, Jack, or Adam and asked one of them if I could meet with them and start working stuff out? I imagine they could help me get my head on straight about you. " At this point, he'd be willing to start seeing a therapist if it would prove to her he was sincere.

Rosemary nodded. "Yes. But if you're going to do it, you've got to put your heart in it because I'm *done* warring with you. When you get like you were at the store today, the bitch in me comes out with her claws bared. Having Wes watching us go at each other like that makes it even more painful. I don't see how we can ever be happy the way we're going right now. Something needs to change."

Evan felt hope kindle in his heart again. "So you'll give me another chance?"

Rosemary shook her head. "No. I'll give *us* another chance because I'm just as responsible for losing my temper. We have to change something. I know it was love that motivated you this morning, but it was love mixed with pride. I let my mouth run wild right back at you because of my injured pride and embarrassment. We were both wrong."

"Rosemary is right. Sometimes it's like we're still in fifth grade. We're supposed to be in love." Wes gestured between Evan and Rosemary. "*You're* supposed to be in love."

Rosemary sniffled and nodded then released their hands and rose from the chair. She searched through the cabinet above the coffee pot for some acetaminophen and took a couple then made her coffee.

Observing her, Wes asked, "You have a headache, baby?"

Returning to her chair, Rosemary nodded. "Yes, since lunchtime. It was better earlier, but now it's pounding again. The coffee might help."

Wes stroked her shoulders and neck, catching Evan's eye. She closed her eyes, and he rubbed more thoroughly. "It's the stress. Why don't you let us rub your shoulders and back? I'm sure it will help your head. If you stayed the night, I know you'd sleep well on your new bed. You'd feel all better in the morning." Wes leaned forward and kissed her temple, gesturing with his chin for Evan to come closer. Evan wasn't so sure this was good timing, but she seemed receptive.

Rosemary's eyes popped open, and she chuckled. "You want me to stay so you can take advantage of me." Wes scooted closer on his chair and drew her into his lap. Evan took a position on her other side.

Wes kissed her temple again. "I won't deny that we want you, baby."

As Evan swept the hair from her neck and kissed the hollow behind her ear, he murmured, "Let us love you like men instead of boys, and I'll bet some things would change between us."

"You make a fine argument, Evan," Rosemary murmured.

His self-discipline was rapidly fading as he nuzzled the silky spot beneath her ear. Her resolve seemed to be fading, too. Was that what she'd waited for? That realization?

Evan wanted to be sure she knew she had options if this progressed farther. "At least let us rub your back and shoulders, see how it goes from there. If you don't feel right about it, just tell us and everything stops." Rosemary looked at him and appeared a little surprised. Yep, Wes wasn't the only one who could be the voice of reason.

Her eyes slid closed as he brushed his lip along her jawline and sighed. "I suppose I could," she replied, and Wes smiled with triumph and relief at Evan over her curly-topped head.

Wes tilted her chin up and kissed her tenderly. "You remember what it was like the first time? We love you even more now, if that's possible. We're more experienced, and we'd make you feel good, baby."

Evan's cock swelled in eager agreement, and he was grateful that Wes had brought it up. Making love to Rosemary was and had been tops on his fantasy to-do list for years. Rosemary moaned as Evan pressed his chest against her back and stroked her hips.

"Good is an understatement. But don't remind me you're more experienced. You're mine, and I don't want to share anymore." The steely tone of her voice was different, new to them, almost dominant. Wes's nostrils flared, and Evan's cock grew even harder against her at that utterance. If she wanted to claim them for her own, they were more than willing to oblige her. She looked from one to the other. "I'd like that back rub, if you wouldn't mind, but I want to shower first."

Releasing her, Wes said, "We'll meet you in your bedroom. There's massage oil in your bathroom."

Rosemary tilted her head at his statement. "You bought me massage oil?"

Evan nodded, glad she seemed pleased. "Yes. We got you some things from Madeleine's in case you needed them."

Her eyes twinkled mischievously. "Oh? Just in case, huh?"

Evan grinned. "We believe in being prepared." He thought of the bottle of lubricant and naughty little toy in her night table drawer that she probably hadn't seen yet. Yeah, they were a couple of Boy Scouts, always prepared.

"All I have here is a robe."

"Wear it if you want to. We'll only uncover what you want us to rub, and you don't have to take it off until you're ready." Evan kissed her shoulder, hoping to reassure her. "We want you, Rosemary, all of you. But not unless you're really ready for us."

* * * *

An ache had been growing and intensifying in Rosemary's body, their words and the timbre of their voices doing magical things to her insides. Evan's words made the muscles in her pussy draw up as if they'd been plucked by unseen fingers, and his touch drew a rush of moisture there. Evan and Wes retreated quickly to their bedrooms to shower as well. Walking down the hall to her bedroom, she felt the dampness spreading to her outer lips. Hearing the showers come on in the men's bathroom, she stripped her clothes from her body. She'd held off from making love with them, waiting for the right time. Now, she finally gave herself permission to live in this moment, however it turned out.

The hot shower felt so good on the tense muscles of her shoulders. Standing under the spray for at least five minutes, she reveled in the sensation of all the jets in the multiple shower heads. There was motivation enough right here to move in tomorrow. The shower was big enough for three with enough shower heads so that no one was left in the cold. Rosemary heard a knock at the bathroom door, and Evan's dark head poked in.

"You okay in here? Need anything?" Evan asked.

"Actually, I could use shampoo and a bottle of body wash. I didn't look before I got in."

"Can I come in? I'll get it from the linen closet for you."

"Sure. But I'm *nekkid*," she replied with a giggle.

"Mmm, you tempt me, woman." Evan's resonant voice sent a bolt of heat straight to her clit. At this rate, they'd have the robe off and her legs spread before she even got to the bed. He brought it to the foggy glass door of the shower and tapped with his knuckle.

"Here you go."

Sliding the door open, she could see that his hair was wet, and his lean hips were wrapped in a bath towel. The towel did nothing to hide his stiff cock, which stood at attention. Biting her lip, she slid the shower door open farther, taking in the sight of him as she offered him the same courtesy. At his groan of appreciation, she glanced up into his bedroom eyes and absently took the bottles he offered. His turbulent brown eyes were half closed, and she'd have to be blind not to see the love and desire that glowed there. The muscles in his jaw looked tense, like he was gritting his teeth together.

Rosemary watched, entranced, as he reached a hand out to her. A whimper escaped her when the back of his knuckles traced the underside of her breasts, stroking from one to the other over her damp skin. Turning his hand, he cupped her left breast and stroked his callused thumb over her peaked nipple. His raspy touch sent fiery tingles from her nipple straight to her cunt. Even with the hot water running over her, she felt the heated rush of moisture that flooded her pussy, causing her lips to swell in eager arousal at his touch. He removed his hand as if he'd awoken from a trance.

"Sorry, I'll let you finish."

Shakily, she whispered to him, "I'll be done in a few minutes."

"We'll be in the bedroom."

Before she slid the glass door closed, she said, "You're good for a girl's ego, honey."

"My pleasure," he murmured and exited the bathroom. Closing her eyes, she felt the magnetic pull from the bedroom. She moaned as she recalled his touch, and her body flared with aching desire. Her hands shook as she poured the shampoo and smiled at the slow, burning anticipation that flared between her legs.

When she was ready, she stepped from the bathroom into the walk-in closet and slipped into the sheer, black lace robe she'd placed in there earlier in the day. Feeling sexy as she went into the bedroom, she saw the interest flash in her men's eyes. Maybe they were expecting a robe that actually covered her up? She savored the sight of them lying diagonally on her bed, both their hips wrapped in towels, their twin erections unmistakable underneath.

The thought of being penetrated by both at the same time sent a spear of raging lust to her pussy, and her inner muscles clenched in need of being filled.

A bath sheet lay flat in the center of the mattress, where they wanted her to lie down.

"How does your head feel?" Wes asked as he patted the towel and helped her into position.

"It's a lot better. I love that shower so much."

Wes replied, "I'm glad it helped. We have showerheads like those in our shower, as well. They really help on tense muscles."

"I think talking things out helped, too. I'm so relieved I'm practically euphoric," she said as she climbed onto the bed.

Wes chuckled. "Hmmm. Evan and I haven't even gotten started yet. Let's get this pretty thing off." Wes stroked her breast as he slid his fingers under the lacy edge of her robe. She nodded, kneeling between them. They untied the robe and pulled away the lacy, ruffled edges over her shoulders, revealing her naked flesh underneath. Her cheeks grew hot at the dreamy, appreciative smiles on their faces, and she heard one of them growl low.

"Wes, look at her bare little pussy."

"I'll bet she's as smooth as silk. Baby, that's the prettiest sight. I love your pussy waxed bare."

"I prefer it that way, too. Glad you approve." More heat blossomed in her pussy as she watched their eyes glaze over a little with lust. Self-consciously, she licked her lips.

Wes's erection twitched beneath the towel around his hips, and she heard him groan in response.

Evan drew the robe away from her and whispered, "Why don't you lie down and get comfortable?" She noticed he bit his lower lip as he looked her nude body over.

Both men lay down on either side of her and stroked her with their soothing, work-roughened hands. As his hand caressed her abdomen, Wes murmured in her ear, "Baby, with you naked like this, we're going to be hard pressed to not make love to you tonight. Are you sure you want this?"

"I still want my massage," she said, giggling playfully as she turned onto her stomach. "But I want more, too. I won't expect you to stop. You, too, Evan. I love you, and I want to be yours tonight."

"You're trembling," Evan murmured, his hand smoothing over her shoulder blade and down her back, setting off a flurry of shivers. "Are you sure?"

She nodded then replied, looking up into Evan's eyes, "It's a big step. Once I have you, I don't see how I could give you up. If I lose you, it'll break my heart, and that scares me."

Evan leaned forward and brushed his full lips against hers. "We're yours, Rosemary, now and forever. We only want to love you and make you happy."

As Wes kissed her shoulder, he whispered, "Get comfortable, baby, and let us rub your back. We'll see what happens."

Chapter Eight

Wes smiled at Evan when Rosemary closed her eyes and got comfortable. He poured the massage oil into Evan's hands and his own. A light, citrus scent filled the air as they smoothed the oil on her creamy skin, starting at her shoulders.

Wes observed Evan, mirroring his motions across her shoulders and up and down her spine to her lower back. It pleased him that Evan went slowly and took his time stroking her. Wes grimaced when she moaned as they reached a reactive spot above her tailbone that made her arch her back and tip her ass up slightly.

Taking it slow, they massaged every inch of skin, including the arches of her feet and her toes, which made her moan again. Wes noticed Rosemary was panting quietly when they parted her legs and worked their way back up to their true destination. Wes glanced at Evan, and they stopped short of touching the slightly opened, wet lips that lay at the juncture of her thighs and firmly massaged her derriere first, drawing extra blood-flow through the area to make her more sensitive for their lovemaking. Rosemary groaned in bliss, showing she enjoyed each steady, solid stroke by tilting her sweet little ass up into their hands. Wes groaned as further evidence of her pleasure seeped in droplets from her pussy. He looked up and noticed Evan's eyelids slide shut as he clearly fought for control.

Wes got Evan's attention before going further, gestured at his mouth, and held up one finger. He pointed at Evan and held up two fingers then pointed at her. This let him know Wes wanted to taste her pussy first but Evan would be the first to make love to her. Evan smiled and nodded, looking grateful. Jack had suggested they develop a system so they could communicate non-verbally when making love to her. That way she didn't have to listen to them jockey for position, thus ruining the mood.

Wes patted her ass and said, "We're going to turn you now, baby, and finish your massage. So far so good?"

Rosemary replied with a sexy, affirmative sound and turned on the bath sheet for them. Her cheeks were rosy, and she looked more than a little aroused, if they were judging by her hardened nipples and the breathless quality of her voice. Wes noticed she was wet, her bare lips flushed and pink, and slick moisture flowed from her cunt. Her hips undulated as Evan's fingertips stroked her abdomen briefly.

Evan groaned and closed his eyes, swallowing convulsively. Wes noticed both of their hands were shaking now. She gazed up at them with half-closed eyes. He poured more oil in Evan's hands and his own and then rubbed them together.

Rosemary asked, "That's a pretty scent. What is it?"

Evan checked the bottle. "It's Orange Blossom. I'm glad you like it."

Rosemary sighed as they smoothed the oil over her abdomen and down the fronts of her legs before massaging it in. Once they reached her toes, they reversed, working slowly up her inner calves and thighs. They rubbed her upper chest and shoulders then worked it into her abdomen and belly. Each man smoothed the oil upward and over the swell of her full breasts, mirroring each other's movements, saving her peaked, rosy nipples for last. Rosemary cried out and shuddered when at last they touched them with their finger tips, panting as they continued. Judging by the sexy sounds she made, she wanted to come already, and they hadn't even touched her pussy yet.

Wes nodded at Evan and grinned when Evan rolled his eyes in relief, and they both bent down to her nipples. Crying out sharply when their mouths closed over her nipples at the same time, Rosemary arched her back into them, increasing the pressure as their tongues laved over her succulent flesh. As he suckled on her nipple, he felt her slide her hand around his bicep and hold on to him. Wes hoped she knew he wanted to be there for her to hold on to, always. Her panting cries increased, and after a minute, they both finally released her with a light pop.

Licking his lips, Wes murmured, "Rosemary *tastes* like orange blossom now, too, doesn't she, Evan?"

Evan sounded in need as he replied, "She sure does. I could make a meal out of her."

Their hands strayed down to her hips, and she shuddered adorably then whimpered in anticipation. Wes lightly feathered his fingers over her mound at the top of her slit. Rosemary hissed at the contact and held on to his bicep harder, and he could feel her trembling. Wes stroked lightly over her silken, damp outer lips, teasing her slit as Evan bent down to her and kissed her lips, stroking her lower lip with the tip of his tongue until she parted them for him.

Wes lifted one of her smooth, silky thighs, to move between them, and fingered her inner lips, which were pink and swollen. Her scent rose to his nostrils and made his mouth water for a taste of her, but he held off. He wanted to explore and knew he wouldn't be able to take just one taste. Parting her delicate lips, he could see her clitoris was also engorged and begging for attention. He could hear Evan whispering to Rosemary between kisses. Wes petted her cunt and stroked a single finger into her opening before retreating, teasing her again as she groaned against Evan's lips. Wes tortured her with light, little caresses until she moaned in frustration. Rosemary shuddered in bliss when he slid two fingers into her snug little pussy and began a slow pumping rhythm. Her hips flexed against him in trembling counterpoint to the motion, and he felt her pussy draw tighter on his fingers.

"Baby, do you want to come?" he asked, placing a light peck beside her satiny bare mound.

She broke Evan's kiss long enough to whisper, "Yes, please, honey. It feels so good."

Evan latched on to a nipple and teased the other with his fingertips while Wes lowered his mouth to her mound. Reverently, he slid the tip of his tongue over the seam of her slit and tasted the hot, silky flesh inside it as her juices seeped for him and she moaned his name.

Wes remembered their first time together and how he'd stroked her with his tongue like this, making her come several times before she'd finally begged him to take her. Turning his head, he delved in more greedily and slid two fingers into her cunt again and resumed the pumping motion. Rosemary moved wantonly against him, moaning their names when he delivered a series of light flicks to her swollen clit.

Evan kissed her and whispered in her ear how much he loved her, how much they loved her as Wes delivered heavier strokes over her clit with his tongue. Her movements became more focused and urgent, and the muscles in her pussy gripped his fingers. She was close to orgasm.

Ready to deliver the final push, he licked her clit once more then closed his lips around it and sucked gently. Rosemary's back arched, and she was motionless for a second. He felt her orgasm break over her in a beautiful, pulsating rush. A long, sobbing wail erupted from her throat as her body undulated against his fingers, and her creamy cum spilled onto his fingers.

While Evan kissed and caressed her, Wes stroked her pussy until he was sure she was done. He came to her and lay down beside her as she turned her face to him and kissed his lips. Giving him a sexy, satisfied smile, she said, "So that's what I taste like when you make me come?" Evan groaned at her words, and Wes nodded as he licked his fingers.

He kissed their naughty girl and said, "Evan, you have to taste her pussy. It's the sweetest thing, and you won't believe what she tastes like. I had to think about it for a minute," he said with a mischievous grin. "Baby, will you let Evan taste your pussy before he makes love to you?"

* * * *

Rosemary smiled at the eagerness in Evan's eyes and nodded. Evan kissed her lips once more before moving between her open thighs. He took his time like he planned to be there a while. He lifted her legs, bent at the knee, and pushed back slightly so she was wide open to his gaze, and her pussy pulsed at the pleasant thought. She felt laid bare by the heat of his gaze and the vulnerability of the position. Rosemary loved knowing he was in charge of the moment.

"Mmm, beautiful. What a pretty, little bare pussy you have," Evan murmured straightforwardly and kissed the space at the juncture between her mound and thigh then slid his tongue straight up her slit.

Rosemary cried out at the sudden stimulation on her sensitive flesh. Wes stroked a nipple with his fingertips as he feathered kisses along her collarbone. Both men grinned happily at her outcry.

"Did you like that, Rosemary?" Evan asked, smiling devilishly before feasting greedily on her pussy. Wes was all finesse. The slow, erotic buildup to the ecstatic explosion that left her quivering and sated. Evan's technique was more of a sneak attack that she had a feeling was going to culminate in an eruption of volcanic proportions.

"Oh! Yes, so much!"

The pleasurable, rippling spasms that signaled the arrival of her orgasm had begun to shiver through her pussy when Evan suddenly switched gears. He smiled wickedly at Rosemary's whine of frustration and stroked her slowly and lovingly with his tongue, which sent her flying higher and higher. She moaned his name when he slipped first one, then two fingers inside her pussy. Her pussy muscles grabbed on to him, and she knew Evan could feel her trembling in anticipation.

"Oh yes, honey!" she cried out when his talented fingers found her sweet spot. She flew even higher. Her muscles felt like they were squeezing his fingers impossibly tighter.

In a gravelly voice that made her pussy quiver, Evan murmured, "I can't wait to be inside you, Rosemary. To feel you squeezing my cock like you're gripping my fingers right now. You're trembling. You must want more." Evan stroked her clit with his thumb while he massaged her G-spot. The joyous, inevitable slide to orgasm took hold, and she moved uninhibitedly with the certainty of it.

Wes hummed in pleasure as he stroked her breast. "She loves it, Evan. Look at her beautiful smile. Would you like more, Rosemary?" Wes didn't wait for an answer as he latched on to her nipple with his hot mouth and suckled with more urgency, escalating the pitch of her panting moans.

"Evan!" was all Rosemary could manage as she moved with him. Her eyes slammed closed, and she threw her head back as Evan lowered his mouth to her mound once again and whispered against her pulsating flesh.

He flicked her clit firmly with the tip of his tongue and bore down on both sides of it with his lips over his teeth, gripped it firmly, and flicked some more.

Rosemary's body bore down harder, and she screamed rapturously, her orgasm rushing through her body in wave after mind-numbing wave of ecstasy. Her cream flooded her pussy as she rode his fingers and lips. She experienced a mini-orgasm when Evan growled against her clit as he lapped her cream from her. She caught her breath as he continued to lick and nuzzle her, sliding his fingers from her pussy when she was finished and gazing at her, a positively primal glint in his dark eyes.

"Figured it out, didn't you?" Wes asked, stroking her abdomen with gentle fingertips, causing her to quiver. Evan nodded as he released her thighs and looked into her eyes. He seemed filled with tension as she stretched and smiled blissfully at him. She realized at some point he'd removed the towel from his hips as she was able to finally see his cock for the first time.

Evan was beautiful, and he was hers. It was so thick she would barely be able to wrap her fingers all the way around it, and wonderfully long and hard. A happy sigh escaped her as she touched him for the first time. He groaned when she took him in her hand and stroked his length. His cock was hot and very hard, indeed.

Stilling her hand, Evan murmured, "I want to last for you. Keep doing that and I'll embarrass myself."

Evan stroked her left thigh and lifted her knee to his side, positioning the blunt head of his cock so that her fevered wet entrance kissed it greedily. She pressed back against him trying to take him inside her.

Lowering his lips to hers, Evan kissed her deeply then nuzzled her lips, holding his position outside her entrance. "I want to be your man, Rosemary. I'm done trying to control you and crowd you into doing things my way. I want to be a man you'd be proud to call yours." His voice was a rich, resonant caress, and his words were a balm for every hurt he'd ever caused. Arousal built inside her explosively, and she tilted up for his kiss again, her fingers cupping his cheekbones.

For a few seconds, she gazed into his eyes, wanting to remember this moment forever. "We've waited a long time, Evan," she whispered, her eyes overflowing and heart pounding as he lifted her to him and pressed his thick, hard length home. She arched her back as he held her to ease his access, and he thrust firmly into her tingling pussy. They both moaned ecstatically as he thrust again and again until he was deep inside her, every inch of his length engulfed. She was consumed with the sensation of Evan inside her for the first time. It had been a long, long time, and her pussy tingled because he filled her so tightly.

In all the years she dated, no other man, besides these two, had ever made her feel this way. Rosemary had dated some genuinely nice guys and even played around with them a bit. But none of them had been able to offer Rosemary what she needed. When she gave herself, she didn't want it to be a casual thing, so Rosemary had held out for something that would last forever. For that reason, this was only the second time she'd ever made love, and she now felt completely justified in having waited. She felt like she'd truly given herself to them.

Wes stroked her cheek and the thigh she clasped around Evan's hip, whispering love words in her ear. In the past, she'd wondered what it would be like, the first time they were all in bed together. Would one of her men feel left out? Wes grounded her and let her know he was there loving her, touching her. When access allowed for it, he kissed her, nuzzled her, or played with her nipples, but he never interfered with Evan. His hands on her, plus Evan's, intensified the sensations and overwhelmed her in a good way.

Evan whispered against her throat, "How are you doing, Rosemary? Am I hurting you?"

"Hu–hurting me?" she squeaked, amused because she could feel her pussy growing slicker around him. "Um, no, honey. What you're doing right now is the exact opposite of hurting me. I'm *good*," she added with a sinuous undulation of her hips and strongly gripped him with her pussy muscles in appreciation. The extra slipperiness increased her range of motion as she tilted against him.

"Holy shit, that felt incredible!" he rasped, carefully lowering his torso to hers and settling himself. She gripped his ass cheeks as she squeezed his cock again. "It feels so good when you do that. I've got to move, Rosemary, I hope you're ready."

Rosemary smiled at him. "Don't hold back, Evan. Do it like you've wanted to for so long." She moved with him, against him, as he thrust. Lying back, she clasped her legs around his hips and permitted him to take control. Wes moved beside her, and she felt his hands in her hair. She entwined her fingers with Wes's and turned to him for a kiss.

Continuing to move with Evan, Rosemary squeezed his cock with her pussy muscles when he pulled out, watching the rapture on his face build with each thrust back in. He smiled at her and sat up on his haunches and tilted her hips, lifting her to him, and stroked again. The change in position brought his cock into direct contact with her G-spot with each perfect stroke, and her lips were stretched out over his cock so that her clit collided with his pubic bone on every thrust, as well. The combination was incredible, and she panted and cried out.

"Evan found your sweet spot, didn't he, baby? Is he stroking it good?" Wes asked, smiling at her as he watched her experience such blissful ecstasy.

"It—it's so good. I'm, oh!"

Evan grasped her hips and thrust more powerfully, hitting her clit and her G-spot with every ingenious stroke.

Urging her on, Wes said, "Yeah, he's making it good for you, isn't he?"

She hoped they'd understand her incoherent words. "I! Oh, so good. Honey, don't stop! So—Mmmhmmm!"

With each strong thrust, the muscles in her pussy gripped him harder, and she knew she'd come again soon. Her pussy flooded with her hot juices.

"You feel so fucking good. That's it, Rosemary, let it go!"

Keeping eye contact with Evan, she watched his face reflect awe as pure joy radiated from her. Rosemary cried out as her orgasm crashed over her and her pussy convulsed around his cock. Evan thrust hard three more times before he finally stilled and let loose a guttural groan as his release found him. His pulsing cock filled her with his cum as he ground several more times against her clit. His movements and her undulating rhythm increased, and she cried out as she came for him again.

Chapter Nine

The hot, sweet tug of her silken pussy on Evan's pulsating shaft was beyond belief. Since Rosemary was on the pill, condoms were unnecessary. Being skin-on-skin with her was pure heaven. *Holy fuck! Where had she learned that little trick, squeezing and tugging on his cock on every stroke? It had about killed him!*

"I must've died because that was heaven," Evan murmured, gazing into her luminous eyes. He still sat on his haunches, holding her hips to him. "You're the prettiest thing, with your rosy cheeks and your eyes glowing like that, with my cock still inside you. I love that," he murmured as he watched his still semi-erect shaft slide from her, covered in her juices and his own cum mixed together. "Damn, this is the sweetest pussy."

She smiled then gasped as his fingers petted her, stroking her clit and swollen, pink inner lips. "Beautiful," Evan whispered, looking into her eyes, making sure she knew he was referring to the whole package and not just the little bit of heaven between her legs.

"Thank you," she replied, kissing him as he moved to her other side, opposite of Wes, who was quiet. Rosemary turned to Wes and asked, "Wes, honey? Are you all right?"

A slow smile spread across his lips. "I'm a *damn* sight better than all right. That was incredible, watching the two of you make love to each other. The most erotic thing I've ever seen or experienced. Until now, making love as a threesome was all theory. I was never sure how I'd react until we actually did it. It was a huge turn-on, watching Evan sink his cock into that luscious, wet pussy of yours." Wes paused and rubbed his hand on his chin. "The sight and the sound of it, watching him slide in and out of you, watching the tension in your body build then explode like that. Baby, it was beautiful. I'll never forget this night. It's been unbelievable, and I haven't even made love to you yet."

Evan enjoyed being the one making love to her, but he could admit to a fantasy or two about watching her make love with Wes, as well. Thinking about it meant visualizing it, and of course, his cock reared up and seconded the motion.

Rosemary stroked his chest and said, "No, you haven't. But I'm ready, if you want to?"

Echoing Evan's concern, Wes asked, "Are you sore? Sure you're up for one more round?"

Rosemary nodded. "I may be a little sore in the morning, but I think that's understandable. I want—need—both of you tonight. Please?" Evan chuckled at the way her bottom lip pouted a little and she used that cajoling tone, and then the naughty girl kissed her finger and licked it then stroked the head of Wes's stiff, distended cock. His brother groaned and closed his eyes.

"I never want to disappoint you, baby. How do you want to do it?" he asked, arching a brow playfully.

She gasped happily. "I get to choose?"

"Sure you do. Man on top, woman on top, rear entry, whatever you want."

Evan grinned indulgently at her as her cheeks returned to their earlier rosy color, and her nipples turned to hardened little peaks. "Can I be on top?" she asked. The innocent yet excited way she asked sent a shot of lust straight through his cock to his balls, and he was hard all over again.

"Sure, baby." Wes moved to the center of the mattress and propped himself up on pillows then reached for Rosemary. Evan helped her straddle Wes's thighs. His brother's cock stood up at rigid attention, a drop of pre-cum escaping from the slit. Rosemary surprised them both when she licked her lips and reached for both their cocks and began stroking them.

Evan had expected to slip into the role of voyeur by this point, but Rosemary clearly had other plans. Evan's cock was still wet with her juices and once again rock hard. Her fingers slid up and down his slick shaft as she licked her lips then went down on Wes, licking the droplet from the head and moaning happily like she wanted more. Evan's cock throbbed in her hand as Wes moaned when she swirled her tongue around the wide, ridged head of Wes's cock. Closing her lips over the slit in a kiss, she slowly slid the head between her lips, giggling at his groan of pleasure. Rosemary tongued the head then slid her lips down, taking his cock to the back of her throat.

Evan surmised she must've sucked on her way back up because Wes groaned in ecstasy.

"Oh fuck!"

Even with her mouth full of cock, Evan could tell by the twinkle in her eyes that she was smiling. After taking a second to lick her palm, she continued stroking Evan's cock, using the same rhythm as with Wes. Evan couldn't wait to be on the receiving end of her tender, loving care.

Rosemary licked the underside of Wes's cock, and he moaned another expletive. Using the same up-and-down rhythm, she suckled for another minute then switched to licking and tonguing his balls, which Wes sounded like he enjoyed as well. She needed her other hand to steady herself, so Evan continued stroking his cock.

Evan watched her as she paid attention to his brother and was blown away by how much he enjoyed the erotic freedom of the moment. Rosemary was on her hands and knees with her little ass stuck up in the air, going down on his brother like it was the only thing in the world worth living for. Her blush had spread from her cheeks to her breasts and down her torso. Even her ass was a light rosy color. Unable to resist such tempting fruit, Evan skimmed a hand over her ass to her cleft. She moaned happily when he slid his fingers over her pussy and discovered that she was dripping wet again.

"I see what you mean, Wes. This is totally hot, watching what she's doing to you. We are such lucky bastards. Rosemary, we're going to make you so happy you'll never want to leave." Evan hoped like hell that was a promise he could keep.

She squealed when Evan slid his fingers into her cunt and petted her, coating them in her cream before returning that hand to his cock. The slick, sweetly-scented lubrication was the last straw for his cock as he tugged in earnest. Wes's features contorted in ecstasy and Rosemary undulated with her movements. Her cunt was swollen and wet, ready to be filled. Evan stroked himself to another orgasm, grinning at the tortured, ecstatic sounds his brother made.

* * * *

Rosemary noticed the deep, gravelly tone of Wes's voice as he spoke. "Evan, while she's on her hands and knees, why don't you show her the little present we got her last week," Wes said before groaning when she suckled on the head of his cock again. Rosemary cooed over his cock as she licked him, wondering what kind of naughty little present they'd gotten her. She heard a drawer on the night table being pulled open then heard the snap top on the bottle of lubricant she'd seen in there a few weeks ago. Evan slid his hand down her spine, over her ass, to her cleft. Tilting her hips up, she cheekily waggled her ass at Evan.

"Did you see that, Wes?"

"I damn sure did. You're a playful thing tonight."

She giggled over Wes's cock then released him with a pop and said, "You wouldn't do anything I wouldn't like."

"You're right, baby. This may be a little cool at first," Evan answered, parting her outer lips. Rosemary heard a little noise and then felt a small vibrator being inserted and held between her inner lips. She shuddered in pleasure at the sensation, incredibly turned on with Wes's cock in her mouth and a vibrator between her legs. She rubbed her pussy against Evan's hand holding the vibrator. His soul patch tickled her skin as Evan bestowed warm kisses on her ass cheeks, and he moved so close behind her she could feel his hot breath on her pussy. While he continued to stimulate her with the vibrator, Evan licked and kissed her cunt, moving slowly from her clit and past her opening.

Rosemary gulped hard when she felt his tongue moving over her perineum to her asshole. Everything below her waist seized up into a tense knot, centering between her legs. Never would she have thought that either one of them would do *that* to her. She screamed in shock at the raw, taboo ecstasy of his hot tongue rimming her asshole. All those sensitive nerve endings came roaring to life. She released Wes's cock for a moment, unable to keep quiet.

"No! Oh God, yes!" she howled, writhing at the naughtiness of what he was doing, about to go into orbit as he licked and teased her asshole. He replaced his tongue with a callused fingertip, and she whimpered and panted as he massaged a firm circle around her tight asshole.

Her pussy clenched in need, ready to be filled with more than a vibrator. In her current position, her slick juices dripped copiously down her thigh, and Evan ran his fingers through them before massaging her asshole again.

"Evan!"

"Will you let us both make love to you at the same time someday? One of us in your pussy, the other in your ass?" Every muscle in her body was strung overly taut as if to a bow, about to come violently undone.

Her heart pounded, and she moaned at the overwhelming sensations as her body submitted to his desire. The muscles in her ass gave a little, allowing him entry. She moaned again at the feeling of intrusion, the slight burning as his finger slid farther into her, the feeling of possession that swept over her. Rosemary knew she'd never keep a part of herself back from either of them, even this, if they wanted it. She realized she wanted it, too, much more than she would ever have believed.

"Yes, Evan. Right now, if you want it, honey. I'm yours, all of me."

Rosemary went back to suckling Wes's cock for him as Evan's finger slid deeper. She relaxed into the hot, intrusive sensation of his finger in her ass and a vibrator in her pussy, feeling incredibly sexy and naughty. Her eyes met Wes's, and he held her gaze as the orgasm loomed closer and closer.

Wes glanced at his brother and nodded before murmuring, "I need you too much right now, baby. But soon, we'll slide our cocks into your ass and maybe, if you want it, take you together, as well. Right now, I want to sink my cock into that silky pussy of yours and feel you glove me while I fuck you."

Withdrawing his finger carefully, Evan rubbed her breached hole in a conciliatory sort of gesture, then switched the vibrator off and lay on the bed beside them.

Wes placed her hands on his shoulders, and she rose up while he held his cock in position for her. He hissed when her wet heat slipped over his cock. Considering what a contrast the two brothers were to each other, she would've thought there would be as much difference in the shape and size of their cocks, but they were proportioned almost exactly the same. Long, thick, and guaranteed to please.

Rosemary was eager for his cock but moved carefully at first because she was a bit sore and tingly from Evan.

"Take it slow. That's right, slide on down." Rosemary groaned as she felt him glide into her pulsating opening. Being filled by either of these men was heavenly and so worth the wait. She tilted her hips and circled her pussy around his cock in gradually larger movements.

"Mmm, nice grind, baby. You're a natural cowgirl, aren't you? That's right, tilt your hips and ride it—*Fuck*! I love it when you do-*oo* that." He moaned deeply. "Damn, I missed *you* so much, *all* of you."

Wes wrapped his arms around her hips and thrust firmly, filling her completely. He drew her forward and buried his face in her cleavage and kissed her there then suckled her nipples. She took a few moments to move experimentally, getting the feel of this new position.

"Does it feel good, Wes?" she asked huskily.

"Baby, it feels better than good. You were made to love us. Isn't she incredible, Evan?"

"Beautiful. She moves like a dancer. Are you giving Wes a naughty lap dance?"

Inflamed by Evan's words, Rosemary arched her back, sat up, and started a slow, swiveling grind on his cock. She gripped his cock with her pussy muscles and tugged with each circling motion then alternated with up-and-down pumping strokes.

"Holy shit, she's doing it again!" Wes growled, smoothing his hands over her thighs.

"You're good to us, Rosemary," Evan murmured as he caressed her spine, sending shivers up and down.

Wes thrust upward and groaned. "Sweet as sugar. Evan, why don't you get the vibrator? I'll bet she'd like it now."

Evan switched on the remote and carefully slid it down over her mound. The moment it touched her clit, her pussy pulsated. She heard a sound and realized it was her, panting in high-pitched bursts.

"I'm going to come. Don't stop, Evan. Yes! Harder, Wes!" She could feel the orgasm gaining intensity inside of her, stirring higher and wilder with each second. "I'm coming!" Rosemary cried out and held on to both of them, riding each pulsing wave. Tendrils of deep pleasure spiraled and exploded inside of her.

Wes hissed with each undulation. "Damn, she's milking my cock so hard, fuck! Yes, baby. I love this pussy," he ground out as he grasped her hips and thrust hard several times then stilled with a loud yell. Rosemary felt each erotic pulse of his cock as he filled her pussy with his cum. He thrust into her until her pulses faded, and she toppled to his chest, seeing stars. They caught their breath as Rosemary snuggled on Wes's chest and lay there limp.

She opened her eyes when Evan stroked her back and gazed at him in breathless rapture. When she shivered lightly, he reached for the blanket and pulled it over her and Wes. She smiled and laid her forearm over Evan's chest. He lifted her hand to his lips and pressed warm, wet kisses to her knuckles.

In wonder, she murmured, "I can't believe how lucky I am that you both love me. Thank you."

Stroking her hips with his calloused hands, Wes said, "Let me pull out so you can lie down and get comfortable, baby." She was still folded up over him, her knees at his sides.

Lifting her head, Rosemary gazed into his sated green eyes and said, "Not yet. Please? I need to feel you inside me a little longer. I promise I'll behave." She wasn't ready to be parted from him yet.

Wes chuckled and squeezed her buttocks, saying, "Don't be surprised if I get hard again for you. You have no idea how good you feel, baby. Your pussy is like hot silk throbbing around me right now."

"Mmm, that sounds nice." Rosemary snuggled to him and gazed at Evan, who looked more peaceful than she'd seen him. Ever. Evan smiled sleepily at her and tucked a stray lock of hair behind her ear.

"I love your dimples, Evan. I hope I get to see a lot of them," she said drowsily.

He kissed her hand and said, "I have a feeling you will, Rosie Posie." Rising from the bed to go clean up, he turned to Wes and said, "Rosemary tastes like sweet cream butter."

Rosemary groaned and giggled, appreciating that while Evan might have been thinking it, he didn't mention the nickname he'd used in the past to rile her up. Princess Butterbutt. She had a feeling she'd been upgraded to Princess Butterpussy and was certain that even true love wouldn't stop her from busting him in the kisser if he dared utter it now. To his credit, Evan was wise, as well as intuitive, and kept any further thoughts to himself.

Chapter Ten

Early September...

Rosemary looked into Wes and Evan's eyes in stunned amazement as they knelt in front of her while she sat on the leather couch in the living room. When she'd gotten to the house earlier, her feet had been aching from being on them all day, and her body was so tired she felt like she was numb.

All three of them had been at the hospital until late the night before, worrying about Rachel. Rosemary had not wanted to leave the emergency department waiting room, hoping for news of her condition, finally giving up around midnight and allowing Wes and Evan to take her home to her apartment. She'd gone in to work that day but had been distracted and worried, though relieved that her friend had stabilized. The last she'd heard, Rachel had been moved into ICU after successful surgery to repair her internal injuries from her car accident.

Now, not only did her feet not hurt, she wasn't sure she could feel them at all, she was so taken by surprise. They smiled at her and both placed a hand on her knees.

Once her brain and tongue had gotten together and gained a little traction, she whispered, "You're really asking me to marry you? Are you sure?"

Wes and Evan grinned ruefully at each other and looked back at her and nodded.

"Yeah, baby. Without a doubt, we're sure." Wes slid his hand up her thigh. His gentle grip was reassuring. "You know how much we love you, how much we've always loved you since you were a little girl."

"Yes, but—"

Placing a fingertip over her lips, Wes forged on. "We got derailed for a few years, but we want to make that up to you now. When Grace told us that Rachel was going to be okay, she asked how we were doing. She reminded us that if we've moved on, that we really *should* move on because there are no guarantees in life. If we loved you, we should claim you for our own."

That phrase "claim you for our own" should royally piss her off. Like she was some piece of property they should stake a claim on. The "old" Rosemary would've corrected Wes, establishing for the benefit of all who the "claimer" and the "claimees" actually were. The "new" Rosemary understood what Wes getting at. The truth was the thought made her core tighten up and her heart pound. She even felt her panties dampen slightly.

Wes continued, "We talked with Jack, Ethan, and Adam and got their thoughts on the matter. They agreed, but they urged us to still take it slow and let you take the time you need, to be sure this is what you want. We want you, and we're ready to take that step when you are."

Rosemary smiled at them, placing a palm on each cheek, and said, "Well, I think it's a given that I want to marry you. But how would this work? Legally, I mean?"

She sincerely hoped they'd already worked this one out. Rosemary didn't want it left up to her. Choosing between the two of them was not something she could do.

Evan spoke up without hesitation. "I want you to marry Wes. He sacrificed years of happiness, enduring my pigheadedness and stupidity. He should be the one to say the wedding vows with you. Although, you know those vows will be repeated in my heart, too, don't you, baby?"

"Yes, I do know that."

Evan rose to sit beside her and said, "Besides, he's the oldest. It should be him you marry. I'll draw up papers that make you my heir, the same as you would be if you were my surviving spouse."

"Wow, you both really worked this out. What about a wedding, and, *yuck*, what about my parents?" Wes and Evan knew Rosemary was weary of the ongoing ugliness between her parents. They'd divorced after she left for college. Her mother kept in touch with her, but their visits together always came around to her mother talking about what a bastard her father was. Her father always made his displeasure with her choices in life known on his business visits to the store, speaking to her imperiously as usual, treating her like she was no more than a store employee. They were her only parents, but how was she supposed to do a wedding with parents who couldn't stand the sight of each other and bickered constantly like two juveniles?

With an understanding smile, Wes said, "Well, we're putting you in the driver's seat with regard to the wedding, but *we'd* like to suggest eloping and getting married on the beach somewhere. Name the day and the beach, and we'll be there."

"And there's no pressure for the date. We'll wait as long as you need, Rosemary. Say you'll marry us," Evan held a small jeweler's box out to her in his big, rough palm.

Rosemary's heart was pounding. How many times in her life had she fantasized about this moment, dating back to the first time when she was a little girl making mud pies with these two? Opening the box, she inhaled long and deep as she took her first look at her engagement ring.

It had a smooth, wide gold band with three diamonds, a one carat round-cut diamond, flanked by two half carat round-cut diamonds that sparkled like brilliant fire in their settings. Nestled beside it was a narrower wedding band with tiny, channel-set diamonds that would be soldered to the engagement ring when she married them.

"This is gorgeous, guys. I'm—wow!" she stuttered, speechless.

"Hmm, Rosie Posie at a loss for words? Get the video camera, Wes," Evan joked, but his eyes showed the real emotions in his heart as he slipped the engagement ring from its nest. "Can we put it on you?"

She held out her hand eagerly, and Evan held her trembling hand while Wes slipped it on her ring finger. Wes asked, "Any idea when you want to do this?"

"I'll need to give it some thought. I like your idea about a beach wedding, even the part about eloping. But what about your parents and our friends?"

Rosemary hated the thought of leaving Wes and Evan's parents out because they had no other siblings. It seemed unfair to deny their mom and dad the privilege of being at the wedding, but if their parents came, hers would have to be there as well, or risk their wrath. Either way, they were going to be unhappy, whether they were in attendance or left in the dark. The best option seemed to be letting all their friends and families know where the wedding would be and leave the choice as to whether they came to the individual.

Then the question arose as to which beach they would go to. Wes suggested going to Grand Cayman, and Rosemary loved the idea.

Rosemary groaned when the wedding ceremony and her father's presence came to mind. She laid her head in her hands, searching for a solution.

"What is it, honey?" Wes asked as he stroked her back.

"My dad, the three of us, the logistics." She groaned. "All Daddy will have to do is take one look at our faces and know our true feelings and intentions. He'll never allow it. Mom, I'm not so sure about, but if she's there and he's not invited, she'll gloat, he'll be furious, and we'll never hear the end of it."

"Okay, then I guess we're back to eloping," Evan said as Wes nodded his head.

Wes made a suggestion. "Why don't you talk to Grace, honey?"

"Yeah, it's mainly them, our other friends, and your parents that I'd really want at our wedding, anyway. I'll talk to her about it sometime soon." Grace might be able to help Rosemary put the dilemma into perspective.

Wes smiled and nodded. "Good, honey. Remember, we're not in a big hurry. We don't want you to feel rushed into anything."

"Well, that's fine and dandy, but I have lost time to make up for," she said, grinning at them mischievously. "I feel like celebrating." She giggled as she stood and stripped her top off.

"Anyone care to join me?"

Rosemary laid the top around Evan's shoulders and toed off her red cowgirl boots. After removing her jeans, she threw them over Wes's shoulder as the men both looked on with desire blazing in their eyes. She slipped away from them, clad only in a black silk G-string and a black lace push-up bra. Turning to them as she sauntered from the room, she giggled at the way their eyes followed her sashaying ass as she crooked two fingers at them both to follow.

Chapter Eleven

Rosemary slid her G-string from her hips and stepped from it as she sauntered down the hall. All three of them were bare-ass naked by the time they made it back to her bedroom. Wes and Evan were rock-hard and ready by the looks of their cocks jutting out at her from their groins. Their eyes glittered with lust.

Rosemary heard one of them groan when she presented her ass to them as she slowly climbed onto the bed. The way her pussy was throbbing right now, she felt sure that they could see the glistening evidence of her arousal. Wes climbed onto the bed, slid into position behind her and drew her to recline with her back resting across his chest. This gave him easy access to play with her breasts and torture the sensitive skin of her throat and below her ears with his light, tickling kisses.

While Wes did that, Evan took his time positioning her legs the way he wanted them. She watched the desire and hunger grow in his eyes as he looked his fill of her bare, opened pussy.

"Beautiful." Evan stroked her inner thighs, and she wished he'd touch her where she ached. He made eye contact with her, smiling like he knew what she was thinking, what she needed. His callused fingertips drifted lightly over her sensitive flesh, and her body shuddered in response, quivering against Wes as he held her and stoked the fire growing inside her with his lips and tongue.

Rosemary tilted her head back, every trace of teasing and mischief gone as she gave herself over to the feelings their touches evoked in her. Evan stroked upward over the last few inches of her skin to her pussy, no longer teasing her, instead giving her exactly what she was now begging for.

Growling softly as his mouth joined his fingers at her pussy, Evan stroked with both tongue and fingertips.

Wes murmured to her as he feathered light kisses over her collarbone and up the back of her neck, paying excruciatingly thorough attention to those spots beneath her ears that could reduce her to a writhing puddle of want. His fingers stroked her breasts, cupping them and rubbing over her nipples until her breasts felt swollen and overheated, as well. Between the attention both men paid to her aching, needy body, Rosemary felt the burgeoning assurance of an orgasm.

Evan increased his efforts, flicking and licking her clit with an unwavering intensity that had her wailing. He added another finger to the one already sliding in and out of her pussy. With the added fullness, her pussy clamped down on his fingers, and her back arched off of Wes's chest as hitching cries of rapture erupted from her throat as they both helped her ride the pulses of her orgasm until she was finished.

Somehow through the lovely haze of satiation, Rosemary noticed that the mood had shifted between the three of them. She opened her eyes halfway and gazed into Evan's eyes. Looking at her with an inexplicable mix of rapture and pain in his eyes, he stroked her abdomen before he laid his face on it.

His voice broke as he whispered, "I'm sorry, Rosemary, Wes. So sorry. I was selfish and impatient. How can you allow me to touch you, Rosemary? After the way I hurt you. Wes, how can you want me anywhere near you, much less want me in your marriage?"

Wes placed his hand on his brother's shoulder. "Because I love you, Evan. You're my brother. Because Rosemary loves you, needs you, and can't be happy without both of us. I'm sorry, too. It might have been different if we'd not given in to temptation when you brought Rita home that first time. It felt hopeless then, and we thought the other was all we had left. Our reason for waiting was gone."

Rosemary reached out as Evan turned his face to her abdomen again, clutching her hips. She stroked her fingers through his thick, brown hair then lifted his chin so she could see his eyes.

She knew the blame wasn't all his. "Evan, I'm sorry we gave in to temptation, too. You must've felt like the door had been slammed right in your face. The wasted years are the saddest part for me because I wanted to marry you as soon as we graduated from college. But at least we're no longer wasting time."

"But the biggest share of blame is mine, Rosemary. Because I was a horny, selfish bastard, I forced your hand. Watching you come apart so beautifully for us now, I was struck with how little I deserve to be here *at all*. You never gave up on me. I don't deserve any of this, any part of you. Every moan, every cry from you tonight, I didn't deserve to hear any of them." Her heart throbbed for him, for the guilt she could see in his sincere eyes.

"You and I could debate that point all evening, Evan. But the fact still remains that *I believe* I deserve you. I'm spoiled that way, thanks to you both." She stroked Wes's arm as he caressed the underside of her breast. "I think it's time you fully forgave yourself because we forgive you." Rosemary stroked his cheek with the back of her fingers.

There was a time when she'd fantasized about him coming to apologize with tears in his eyes. She'd dreamed of looking down at him and gloating because he'd finally realized his mistake. Now, she just wanted to move on and forget about the past.

Evan nodded, his head dipping to kiss the top of her mound. He stroked her leg a final time. "I'm going to take a shower. You and Wes can have some time to yourself that way." With that said, he climbed from the bed without having achieved his own release.

Rosemary's brows drew together in concern as she watched Evan stride from the bedroom. A few seconds later, they heard the shower in the other bathroom turn on as they both lay there in confusion.

She turned to Wes and asked, "What? What just happened, Wes? We weren't finished." Stroking Wes's chest, she added, "Not that I mind alone time with you. We haven't had that opportunity yet, but… what just happened?"

Wes inhaled deeply and then released the breath, ruffling her black curls that were still lying on his chest. "Baby, if I had to hazard a guess, I'd say that was a powerful realization, and this is his way of punishing himself."

Rosemary wanted Evan to come back and make love with them, not punish himself because of the guilt he still obviously suffered from. "But I don't need or want that from him. It's been almost two months since we've gotten back together. Why now? Everything has been going so well. Why is he doing this now?"

Wes shrugged and stroked her abdomen with his palm. "I guess he's going to need longer to deal with the guilt he feels. Do you want me to go get him?"

"No, he's started his shower, and I don't want him to feel forced." Looking up at Wes, she added, "But I think I'm going to need to spend some time alone with him. Would that bother you?"

Wes hugged her and caressed her abdomen again, his fingertips slowly tracing down to her mound. "I think we could work out a chance for the two of you to have some time together. You should expect one-on-one attention without having to ask for permission." Wes pressed his lips to her shoulder as his fingertip dipped through the slippery wet folds of her pussy, and she felt herself clutch on his rough fingertip.

"Wes," she moaned

Wes slid a couple of fingers through her wet slit and groaned. "We'll talk about that more, later. Would you let me fuck this little pussy right now?"

"After you asked so sweetly? Fuck me, Wes. That's what I need right now." Sitting up, she allowed him to climb from behind her. She lay back on the pillows, and he moved between her thighs. He looked down at her with raw lust in his eyes as she spread her thighs slowly for him. She slid her foot up his bare thigh before carefully stroking the pads of her toes down his hot, stiff erection. He hissed and pressed her foot against him more firmly.

In a rough, sexy voice he whispered, "Woman, what you do to me." He thrust his erection against her arch. "Incredible."

He grasped each ankle and raised them until her thighs were straight up, her knees slightly bent. He pushed them back until her ass was slightly raised off of the mattress, and then he lowered his face to her dripping wet slit. He growled, and her pussy convulsed again when his hot tongue traced her slit. He teased her clit with the barest hint of contact.

Slowly, he bent her knees farther back to her sides, spreading her so her inner lips parted open, baring every part of her to him, from her hooded clit, to her cream-covered entrance. Wes tilted his head and licked and kissed her pussy lips, and then he rested her feet back on the mattress, lifted her hips slightly, and groaned in bliss as he slid into her flooded pussy until he was sunk to the hilt inside of her. She whimpered in pleasure as he stilled and nuzzled his lips over her neck and down to her collarbone.

"I love your sweet, silky pussy," Wes murmured.

Wrapping her legs around him, Rosemary grasped his shoulders as she slowly undulated on his cock. He slid his forearm under her hips so that his hand grasped her ass then slid the other forearm under her back and shoulders. Doing that increased the pressure his body already exerted on her mound. It also pressed her clit harder against his pelvic bone, and her pussy started throbbing and pulsating. She felt encompassed and consumed by him.

Rosemary held on to Wes as he began thrusting hard, every stroke feeling like it went as deep as it was possible for him to go. She moaned and cried out in sobbing cries as the most mind-bending orgasm she'd ever had loomed over her. His thrusts increased in speed and intensity, and her orgasm rolled over her as she screamed her ecstasy until she was sure his ears would ring for the rest of the day.

* * * *

Evan toweled dry after stepping from the shower. He heard the unmistakable sounds of Wes and Rosemary fucking across the hallway, pausing unashamedly to listen as his bastard of a cock hardened even more. He hadn't touched it while he was in the shower, feeling that he deserved no release for what he'd done to them both. It was sort of fucking stupid when he thought about it. It had been almost two months since their reunion, and he should be over the guilt by now. He thought he was, but it had slammed into him, stronger than ever as she'd screamed her earlier release for him.

He'd realized how little he deserved her cries of pleasure. His cock twitched painfully as he listened to Rosemary peak across the hall. He smiled, able to tell by her sounds that Wes was giving it to her just right.

Her whimpering, sobbing cries gained intensity. The decadent, wet sounds of sex easily heard between her cries. His cock begged and throbbed for a touch, for action of some sort. It was his own fault he felt this way. All those wasted years because his cock needed satisfaction and found it briefly in all the free pussy Rita had initially flung his way.

Evan had fucked Rita every chance he got. It was too late by the time he realized that what she was giving him wasn't satisfying the soul-deep craving inside him. It wasn't Rosemary he was making love to, and it wasn't real love that he was feeling. When he'd finally had that realization, he was already married. He'd trusted Rita implicitly, and while she milked his stupid, ravenous cock for him, she'd also milked him of every penny he'd earned plus incurred debt to satisfy her craving for new things and a grander lifestyle.

He was drawn back to the present as Rosemary let loose with an ear-splitting, rapturous scream. In shameful weakness, he fisted his cock. He could blame the horny bastard all he wanted, but he knew it was connected to his brain and he'd given his self-control over to it. A habit he wasn't proud of. He stroked hard twice, hearing Wes's satisfied roar as he came, and Evan's own cum jetted explosively in stinging, hot bursts, splashing on the mirror and the countertop.

Fucking bastard. He couldn't even give himself the punishment he knew he still deserved. His cock *still* controlled him. Feeling light-headed from his release, he cleaned up the mess he'd made, listening to her sobbing breaths and moans as she cried out with an aftershock. Rosemary was so responsive. She loved them both so much.

He heard Wes's voice as he spoke quietly to her and the soft sound of a wet kiss in the ensuing quiet. He remembered another time, years before, when he'd walked in on them in such a moment. Refusing to intrude on them now, he slipped silently to his bedroom and dressed before moving down the hall and into the kitchen to start supper.

That night, the three of them sat quietly at the kitchen table eating. Evan smiled at the look of bliss on Rosemary's face. Her cheeks were flushed, and she had a happy, peaceful look in her eyes.

Evan could see the questions in her eyes when she looked at him, but even then, she didn't seem put out or worried about his withdrawal from their love play earlier. She seemed accepting of him and his feelings, whatever they were.

There was a time in the past when she would not have been able to let it go. She'd have wanted to hammer it out and pick it apart, pissing him off in the process. Now, she let him have his space and enjoyed her endorphin-induced euphoria. Evan wished for time alone with her so he could be on that page, too.

Wes provided the perfect opportunity when he spoke a moment later. "You know, I've been thinking about the Texas Home Builder's Show in San Antonio at the end of this month. Evan, why don't we get an extra entry pass for Rosemary and bring her along? I checked online, and The Crystal Rose Bed and Breakfast has an opening that weekend. We could make a romantic getaway out of it. Only one of us needs to be at the exhibit booth, anyway, so we could make time to spend alone with her, take her on the Riverwalk or shopping."

Rosemary appeared delighted. "Oh! That sounds like fun." Rosemary turned hopeful eyes to Evan. "I'd love to have some alone time with you. I haven't been to the Riverwalk in years. What do you think, Evan? Could we?"

Evan smiled indulgently at her, knowing full well he'd give her whatever she asked for. "I think it's a great idea. Watching your beautiful face right now, though, I think we might wind up abandoning our exhibit in favor of indulging your every whim. If you think you can get the time off from work, why don't you plan on it."

Rosemary responded enthusiastically, and after the supper dishes were cleared and the kitchen tidied up, they went online and booked the Bridal Suite at The Crystal Rose in the King William District near downtown San Antonio.

Chapter Twelve

Late September...

Rosemary giggled when Wes and Evan groped her ass simultaneously as they followed her into the bed and breakfast bridal suite. "Did you see the look on that woman's face when we left the dining room and headed upstairs together?"

Evan scoffed. "Looked like someone shoved a corncob up her ass."

Rosemary didn't understand why she'd stared so disgustedly at them. They'd behaved themselves like grown, responsible adults, eating in relaxed silence, sharing quiet conversation. No footsy, no hanky-panky, no nothing. Anybody could've watched them as they ate and left the dining room and safely assumed they rented two separate rooms upstairs and not the bridal suite, which comprised the whole third floor. They'd both taken a hand as she climbed the stairs, but that had been their only hint at a threesome.

Wes gazed at her with bedroom eyes as he approached and murmured, "Wait till she hears you scream later when we make you come again and again and—"

"Again," Evan said as he slid in behind her. Wes pressed against her front, enclosing her in their masculine heat.

She couldn't resist the teasing little wiggle that rubbed her breasts against Wes's chest and her ass against Evan's bulging groin. "Hold on, cowboys. Before we get started, I brought a little something along with me that I want to model for you first, after my shower. Do you mind?"

"No, not at all." Wes chuckled. "Just get a move on it. We're randy and ready for you." Then he gave her ass cheeks a squeeze as they released her. She looked back at him and giggled then closed herself in the bathroom.

Sighing happily, Rosemary pulled out the little babydoll nightie she'd hidden on a hanger in the back of her garment bag. She held it up and admired the sheer fabric then hung it on the towel bar before running water in the huge bathtub. Stripping out of the clothes she'd worn on the trip over to San Antonio, she slipped into the steamy water, sighing in contentment.

Wes's voice came through the door. "You all right in there, baby? Need any help?"

"I'm fine. I don't want you to see my little surprise until it's on me. I'll be out in a few minutes." She bathed, giggling at their impatience, then rinsed off, toweled dry, and applied some of the lotion they'd bought for her.

Every time she pictured those two big, strong men standing in the midst of all the girlie lotions, body washes and other potions at Madeleine's Day Spa, sniffing samples, it made her feel special because she knew that was so far out of their comfort zone. They could hover appreciatively over an open can of varnish, extolling its virtues over another. Orange Blossom versus Camellia Sunrise, not so much. She appreciated the effort.

Slipping the sheer babydoll on, Rosemary turned to admire herself in the full-length mirror. It was perfect. The nightie was made from a sheer woven fabric that was embroidered all over with pink roses and had pretty ruffled edging at the hem and satin ribbons for shoulder straps. Her nipples were clearly visible through the fabric and so was her bare mons since she opted to leave the tiny G-string off.

She'd gone to Madeleine's earlier in the week for her regular waxing appointment and was feeling particularly sensitive and sexy in that area, if the moisture that was already seeping from her slit was a trustworthy indicator. After running a wide-tooth comb through her tight curls for a softer, more romantic look, she opened the door. Wes and Evan were already on the bed, undressed and completely ready for her.

Wes spoke as he reached out for her. "Well, don't you look like a little treat. Come here and let us see this little thing you have on."

Evan murmured as she turned for them. "She's wrapped up like a little piece of candy, isn't she?" Rosemary could clearly see their cocks as she came closer. Both men were fully erect and looked ready. Her pussy tingled, and her nipples hardened, standing out against the sheer nightie. Evan's eyes appeared a little glazed as he stared at her bare pussy. She felt sexy and powerful, and her heart soared with desire for them, to please them.

Wes rested his head on his hand and gazed at her with admiration. "Baby, you're lovely tonight. So beautiful."

"Thank you," she whispered. "I'm glad you like it."

Rosemary's heart ached with love for them as they lay there gazing up at her. Candles flickered nearby, casting golden, dancing illumination around the room. Skimming her fingertips over their heavily muscled chests and shoulders, Rosemary trembled with desire when she felt their hands at her thighs as they lifted the hem of her nightie and slowly drew it from her. Hyper aware of the cottony fabric as it slid over her peaked nipples, she lifted her arms so they could remove it and lay it aside. Her pussy ached with desire for them, *both* of them.

Rosemary knew eventually they'd get to that point in their relationship and had gotten together with Grace recently. Grace had talked with frankness to her about having sex with both men at once and what Rosemary could do to prepare herself for it.

Using the plugs the last couple of weeks had helped her get used to the sensation of invasion and to not fight it. Rosemary had found the slight pinch of pain that accompanied the invasion of the lubricated plug in her ass to be incredibly erotic and had enjoyed going about her routine with that pleasant buzz of arousal in the back of her mind.

Gazing into their eyes now, she knew this was that moment. "Would you like to both make love to me together? I'm ready."

Wes and Evan glanced at each other, their faces a delightful mixture of relief and hot desire. *Oh, yeah.* They had a plan all right. Rosemary smiled at their enthusiasm as Wes rose from the bed and returned with a hand towel from the bathroom and a bottle of lubricant from a suitcase.

Evan stroked her ribcage and must've felt her tremble. "Rosemary, are you sure you're ready? We don't want you to feel rushed. You know the idea of doing this with you makes us a little crazy, but we want you to take this step because it's what you want and not because you're having mercy on us. We'll wait as long as we need to."

Rosemary understood the concession that Evan was making by telling her that. She knew how much he'd longed for this with her, not months but literally years. "Evan, I ache with the need to do this with you. Trust me, I don't feel rushed."

"Good, baby," Wes murmured as he returned to the bed. "The last thing we want is to hurt you or rush you through this." Wes laid the items he'd brought with him aside and held out his hands to her, adding, "Why don't you come here and let us love on you a little? We have the whole night ahead of us."

Her whole body vibrating with desire and excitement, all Rosemary could manage was a nod as they laid her down on the pillows piled against the headboard. Evan lay down at her side and feathered his fingertips into the hair at her temple as he leaned in to kiss her.

They were supremely gentle, and she felt like a cosseted little kitten in their arms as they stroked her and loved her.

Wes entwined his fingers with hers at her other side, and she arched when she felt his hot mouth on her breast, drawing on her nipple, creating zinging sensations that raced through every erogenous point in her body, culminating in an explosive throbbing in her pussy.

Rosemary could not imagine what went through their heads when they loved her in such close proximity to each other. Rosemary was impressed that they never reacted to incidental intimate contact as though they were interfering with each other. Their focus always seemed to be working in tandem to reduce her to a writhing puddle of need, with stellar success.

Such was the case now as Evan's lips strayed down her throat and her chest, latching on to her other nipple and suckling side by side with his brother. Her fingers slid into their hair and held them to her, moaning deliciously at the twin sensations tracing through her body as their fingers explored her.

Rosemary lost track of whose fingers slid through the slick moisture at her slit and whose fingers grazed over her thighs, drawing them apart for greater access to her pussy. Their mouths and tongues drew on her nipples with more urgency, lapping and suckling. They drew heartfelt moans from her as their fingers slid into her cunt, stroking and spreading moisture to her clit then paying loving attention there.

Her body was thrown into such a heightened state of arousal by the thought they'd be fucking her together for the first time tonight that she skyrocketed quickly to orgasm. She moved her hips rhythmically with their fingers, and she was surprised by how fast her orgasm swept over her. Their insistent stroking at her cunt kept the climax rolling along until she was completely done. Rosemary loved that about them. They faithfully made sure she was finished, every single time, sometimes keeping her at that point until she came for them again.

Evan leaned over her and crooned, "That's my baby." When the last throbbing pulse subsided, his fingers moved lazily over her mound and her abdomen in a damp trail to her breast. She smiled ecstatically when her pussy quivered in response to Evan's mastery of her body.

During Evan's slow, wet kiss, a low moan of pleasure rose from her throat as she felt Wes's tongue and warm mouth at her pussy. They played her body so beautifully.

She had a feeling if she didn't stuff her fist in her mouth they'd hear her screaming her pleasure all the way down on the ground floor. She hoped when that moment came, over and over again, that she cared enough to make the effort.

Evan released her lips and lay down above her in the bed, a position which gave him free access to her upper body. Wes draped Rosemary's thighs over his shoulders and gazed lovingly at her as he buried his mouth in her pussy, ravenously loving her straight back to the edge.

Stroking her cheek tenderly, Evan whispered, "Wes looks like he's enjoying himself. We love the way you taste, Rosemary. We both sometimes feel like we're starving for you."

She smiled at Wes's growling agreement as he continued driving her higher and higher up the ledge. Rosemary whimpered tremulously when she felt his finger trace through the copious moisture flowing from her pussy then back to her asshole while simultaneously tormenting her clit with wicked flicks of his tongue.

The nerve endings gathered in that little puckered hole screamed to life at his touch, and her body hummed with arousal and the desire to be filled in both places. Her bottom responded to his touch, relaxing as his finger circled in a sensual massage.

Wes slid his tongue into her pussy, and her body tightened at the dual penetration as his finger found access to her back hole at the same time. Rosemary felt a climax bearing down on her. She clung to Evan's arms, her breath coming in uncontrollable pants, her back arching as Wes slid his finger deeper and stroked in and out in a twisting, sliding motion.

Looking down into Wes's eyes, Rosemary saw the love glowing there for her. Her orgasm broke over her hard, and she howled her pleasure loudly. Devouring her pussy greedily, Wes lapped her clit then sucked it between his lips as he continued stroking her asshole, showing no signs of letting up until another climax followed on the heels of the first.

Evan kissed her shoulders and throat as he shifted beside her. As she caught her breath, and for several minutes afterward, they closed in on either side of her and warmed her cooling body with theirs. She appreciated that they didn't rush her through that moment. Their touches were loving and tender, as were the words they whispered in her ears. They never stopped caressing her, and eventually her body began the decadent rise to an even greater degree of arousal as they skillfully stoked her embers.

Trusting them completely, she took Evan's hand when he knelt in front of her and helped her sit up on the bed.

"Ready, baby?" he asked, his eyes radiating desire for her. She noticed Evan's cock twitching at his abdomen, thick and hard for her.

She reached for his cock and looked from him to Wes. "Can I play, too?"

Smiling at their twin groans, Rosemary didn't wait for permission as she bent to Evan's cock and took his hard length in her mouth. He hissed in response as she lapped and sucked the head. Reaching out with her other hand, she stroked Wes's balls and delighted in his strained groan of pleasure. Her fingers strayed through the dark blond curling hairs that covered his scrotum and the base of his cock, and then she slid her fingers around his hardened shaft, stroking up and down slowly.

Evan's needy moan encouraged her as she licked her lips again. He settled back, sitting on his heels, and slid his fingers slowly through her long, black curls. Rosemary took his cock until it bumped the back of her throat then sucked as she stroked back over him, using the same up-and-down motion over Wes's cock with her hand.

"Damn, I can almost feel your mouth on me, Rosemary. That is incredible," Wes murmured.

Humming in response, she continued lovingly suckling on Evan's cock as she stroked Wes's. She enjoyed their reactions to her eager efforts.

She released Evan's cock from her mouth with a pop and wrapped her hand around his cock to placate him as he groaned piteously. She wrapped her lips around Wes's cock and suckled him, as well.

Wes groaned, and his hips surged upward to her as his climax approached, and she sucked harder. She glanced over at Evan, knowing he needed release, too, but with a firmer touch than she was comfortable using. *Quandary.* A mouth full of cock made it hard to communicate verbally, but she couldn't stop. They were both too close for that.

Evan smiled and nodded at the question in her eyes and wrapped his hand below hers. She released him and grasped Wes's cock at the base but kept her eyes on Evan. Evan watched her intently and kept his rhythm the same as her mouth over Wes's cock. She increased her suction and speed, both of her men growling as their orgasms broke over them.

Wes's cum spilled into her mouth in thick streams as she swallowed, while at the same time she felt Evan's cum spill onto her back in hot spurts as he snarled and jerked on his cock hard, his head falling back in ecstasy. She smiled, pleased with her efforts as she licked Wes clean, feeling like she had a mild buzz.

If they were willing to take as good care of her as they did, the least she could do was give them whatever they needed from her. Evan swiped the hand towel over her back, thoughtfully cleaning her up. Rosemary doubted that she would mind if he'd left it there or rubbed it in. Either way, she felt precious to him and wanted by both of them.

Evan lay down on his side, with her between him and Wes. Rosemary took her time kissing both of them, quietly whispering love words meant for them individually. Her heart swelled for both of them as they allowed her to love on them separately for a few minutes.

Wes was relaxed and sexy, allowing her to kiss his chest and lick his nipples while he ran his fingers through her hair. She loved the way they touched her hair, stroking it and running their fingers through it. Evan was quiet, his eyes searching hers, maybe looking for signs of uncertainty over what would come next.

Rosemary finally settled between them, and they cuddled to her, Wes snuggling her to his side while Evan spooned to her back. Rosemary lay sandwiched between, wallowing in their decadent heat and clean, manly fragrances. She reveled in the love that flowed between them, so grateful that they'd been able to overcome their past mistakes. Their fingers and roughened palms stroked all over her, and as she relaxed between them, she felt desire well within her once again.

Normally, she'd be drifting off to pleasant dreams after three satisfying orgasms, but this time she felt further energized. Heat flowed over her from their palms, and she could feel their own desire for her grow as Wes's cock hardened against her thigh while Evan thrust playfully along the cleft of her ass.

She shuddered in little pre-orgasmic shivers at the thought that soon both of those wonderfully hard shafts would be inside her. Their touch became ardent, their stroking more sensual and more intimate as they pressed their cocks to her, growling softly. That sexy sound had her wet in a split second.

Drawing away from her back, Evan reached for the lubricant as Wes drew her to him and rolled to his back, bringing her with him.

"Ready for us to love you together, baby?" Wes whispered to her, nuzzling her cheek. She nodded to him and turned into his kiss, stroking his velvety tongue with her own in a slow, sensuous duel. Evan shifted on the bed, and she felt his fingers slide through the cleft of her ass and the lubricant as he applied some to her asshole and her cheeks.

"Love on Wes for a little bit, Rosemary. You're doing great. I can tell you're trying to relax for me. Thanks, Wes," he added quietly as his finger pressed more lubricant to her opening.

Rosemary looked at Wes quizzically before looking back at Evan.

Wes stroked a lock of hair behind her ear as he replied, "We lost our virginity together. He deserved to have a first with you, too."

Rosemary pressed her lips to her lover's mouth then nodded. "You're the first and only lovers I've ever wanted. The only ones I'll ever need or want."

Evan's hands on her bottom stilled suddenly. "Only?" His voice was muted, reverent.

Wes smirked up at her when she glanced in his eyes. He knew her well and had probably known all along.

"The only ones, Evan," she murmured as she kissed Wes's chest. He smelled so good, manly and sexy.

"Why didn't you tell me? I asked."

"When you asked before, my pride wouldn't let me. I didn't want you to think I was some pathetic loser waiting for nothing."

"Loser? I wouldn't have thought that if I'd known. Wes, did you know?" Evan asked.

"I suspected," Wes murmured as he stroked her hips with his palms. "That made the wait even harder, realizing she was holding herself back from others, waiting for us."

Evan finally said, "You're all ours, aren't you?"

"Uh-huh," she whispered against Wes's chest as Evan's fingers stroked her asshole in slow, thorough caresses, lubricating her well. "Finally yours."

Evan applied lubricant to his cock and spread more on her pussy lips and entrance then wiped his hands on the hand towel. "I want this to be as easy and comfortable for you as we can make it, Rosemary. Lift up for a second."

When she rose up on hands and knees, Evan dispensed the lubricant into Wes's hand. He applied it to his erection, hissing at the contact then pulled her down to settle on top of him. The ridge of his erection was centered between her pussy lips.

Rosemary could not resist grinding on him a little and loved the angelic smile on his face as he closed his eyes and enjoyed the sensation. Then she lifted her ass slightly to Evan's attention.

Wes chuckled at her playfulness and wrapped his arms around her back. He tucked her head under his chin. "Relax now. Plenty of time to play in a minute."

Rosemary mewed at the feel of Evan's fingers sliding into her asshole. The sensation gave her the strong urge to press back against him, but she held still and concentrated on letting him inside her. Rosemary sighed as the muscles gave way then clenched in delight at the naughty, forbidden sensation.

Arching her back, Rosemary willed her body to open for him, giving him greater access. Evan groaned as his finger slipped in all the way and pumped several times, increasing the edgy desire she was feeling, the dark need to be filled with something a little larger there.

She cried out in trembling delight when he added another finger and both penetrated together in a sliding, twisting motion that had her already spiraling toward explosion. Slowing his pace a little, he pumped into her, evidently sensing how high she was already.

When her breathing had slowed down a little and she was no longer perched so close to the edge, he added another finger and continued the same pumping motion, gradually stretching the muscles until they'd allow his cock entrance without hurting her. Wes held her securely, stilling her hips when she would've begun flexing. They must've communicated nonverbally because Wes shifted under her and she felt the head of his cock at her entrance as he lifted her hips over him.

"Ready, baby? I think Evan is dying to slide into your sweet little ass, aren't you, brother?"

"Literally *dying* to slide in. I want you so bad, Rosemary. Wes is going to slide his cock into your pussy." Rosemary could feel Evan's hands on her ass as Wes pressed his cock to her entrance and slid in easily through all the lubricant. Rosemary heard Evan groan in appreciation and realized he was watching from behind as she took his brother's length deep inside her. Wes's cock slid slowly over her G-spot as he held her and rubbed back and forth in that same spot over and over again.

"Wes," she whispered in bliss. Wes smiled at her as she raised her head and kissed him passionately, and then she slammed down on him to the hilt.

Evan chuckled at Wes's tortured groan. "Go easy on Wes, Rosemary. He has to last while I slide in, and I'm going to be going slow. Hold still because I know he wants this to be good for you, too."

"I feel like a teenager with his first girl, baby. He's right," Wes murmured.

Rosemary smiled, and they both chuckled when she said, "I remember a certain young man with his first girl, and he lasted just fine. I think he could probably put most grown men to shame with his prowess." Looking back at Evan, she added, "As can his brother."

Evan's palm caressed her back, and Wes slid his hands down to her ass cheeks and held her open and vulnerable to Evan's big cock. She moaned in aching desire.

Wes muttered torturously, "Damn, I can feel her pulsing around my cock. Rosemary is definitely ready for us."

Rosemary panted as she felt the head of his cock press against her ass for entry. She closed her eyes and relaxed, pressing back a bit against him. His cock felt positively huge. She sighed and released a breath as her ass gave in to him. Evan panted his pleasure as the head slid in a little, meeting more resistance. She took a shallow breath, let it out slowly and simply experienced the intoxicating mixture of pleasure and pain that sang through her body as he slipped farther inside.

Evan's voice was guttural, strained as he spoke. "Oh, fu-uck. She feels so good. Damn, I love this snug little ass. Don't move, baby. I'm trying to slide in slow. I don't want to hurt you. Hold still a minute longer. Oh, fuck!"

Tendrils of rippling pleasure raced up and down her spine, and she mewed as she took more of his cock. The bite decreased, and it was all pure, heady pleasure as he slid farther. Rosemary could feel Evan shaking as he held her. He still went slowly for her sake as she took him all until she felt his hips against her ass.

Evan asked in a gravelly voice, "You okay, baby? I'm all the way in now."

"Uh-huh." Rosemary lay with her cheek against Wes's chest, just *feeling*, unable to speak at the moment. She was afraid if she moved that the thrilling spasms in her pussy would explode inside her and she'd come, screaming like a raving lunatic.

"Amazing," Wes whispered as he flexed his hips and his cock thrust within her ultra-tight passage. She moaned rapturously. It seemed that every part of her was consumed by them.

Evan thrust in concert with Wes's small movements, establishing the rhythm for their lovemaking. Rosemary moaned in pleasure, the depths of her heart in the sound, and her men growled in approval as she undulated between them when she found her place in their rhythm. She braced her elbows on either side of Wes on the mattress and moved in longer strokes between them, drawing groans of ecstasy from them. Evan kissed her spine between her shoulder blades, his lips trailing down as far as he was able as he thrust into her, then grasped her hips in his strong hands. "I'm getting real close, Wes."

"Me, too. Baby, let go for us when you're ready."

"Fuck me," she whimpered and moaned loudly as her hips gyrated wildly between them. The muscles in her overcrowded pussy and ass spasmed in impending climax, and she could no longer control how hard or fast she moved. "Harder, now! Oh God! I'm—"

They grasped her firmly and thrust several more times. Her orgasm broke like a gigantic wave, and she came with a wailing cry as she ground uncontrollably against them both. They roared in ecstasy as their release exploded from them in rapid, pulsing spurts, their hips flexing as they thrust hard. Their cries echoed against the walls before subsiding into sated moans of pleasure.

Rosemary lay motionless between them. A hitching sigh every now and then was the only sound she made. Her eyes were half open as she once more lay with her sweaty cheek plastered to Wes's chest.

Evan caught his breath first and lifted off of Rosemary, stroking her back as he slowly withdrew from her tingling ass. "Be back in a minute, Rosemary."

Rosemary heard the shower come on in the bathroom. Wes caressed her, allowing her to remain motionless with his cock still deep within her. "How do you feel, baby?"

She let out a slow, breathy sigh. "When sensation returns to me, I'll let you know."

Rosemary could hear the concern in his voice. "Did we hurt you? Was it good?"

"Good? It was volcanic. I couldn't understand it until I experienced it for myself."

She heard a rumble of approval in Wes's chest. He sounded satisfied. "We wanted it to be good for you."

She gave him a crooked little grin as she rose up to look in his eyes. "That's like comparing Old Faithful to Mount St. Helens."

Wes chuckled. "It was pretty amazing. You have two men who are devoted to your pleasure," he said, kissing her damp temple.

"I love you with my whole heart, Wes." She smiled as he squeezed her gently, his body trembling a little.

Evan returned, drying his nude body with a towel. Using a hot, wet washcloth, he wiped the lubricant off of her and pressed the soothing heat to her ass, which was throbbing a little. She jumped at first contact but relaxed as he pressed it to her.

"Feel okay? Does that hurt?"

"I'm going to be a little sore, but it's not bad. The heat feels good. I have ibuprofen in my makeup case."

"I'll get them for you. Are you thirsty? You're a little hoarse."

Yep, screaming ecstatically over and over will do that to a girl. They probably heard me at the Alamo.

Chapter Thirteen

Wes chuckled as he ended the call on his cell phone. Rosemary had talked a mile a minute, beside herself with excitement.

Evan looked over at him as the man he'd been visiting with at their exhibit booth excused himself. "Was that Rosemary? Where did she get herself off to?"

She'd admired the large, beautifully landscaped garden area nearby when they'd arrived at the Convention Center earlier that morning and had mentioned that she'd like to take a closer look if they didn't mind. There were plenty of people around, and it was on the beaten path, so Wes and Evan had no objections.

They didn't want her to think they expected her to hang around their exhibit booth the entire time she was there. This weekend was supposed to be a fun getaway for her. On the contrary, they were impressed when, as they'd both been occupied talking to other people, a married couple had approached their booth with apparent interest, and she'd stepped over to them and struck up a conversation, answering their questions and showing them samples. Rosemary had winked at Wes when he'd caught her eye, and he'd had to work hard to focus on what the contractor was saying to him.

It filled him with pride that she took an interest in their business, and it came as no surprise that she would be perfectly comfortable talking with potential customers since sales were a big part of what she did in her job.

Later when the traffic at their booth had tapered off a bit, she asked if they'd mind if she took that walk outside. That had been half an hour ago.

Wes nodded, smiling. "Yeah, it was Rosemary. She took her walk outside, but it started drizzling. She came in a different door from the one she went out of and got all turned around and wandered into a different part of the Convention Center."

Evan's face showed mild concern. "She get lost?"

Wes grinned. "No. I wouldn't say lost. More like she's found Wonderland. She wandered into another convention going on somewhere else in this facility."

"Oh yeah?"

"Yeah, it's open to the public, too. Remember that line of people we saw when we were pulling up? She's with all of them right now."

"What are they here for?"

Wes grinned and chuckled. "The Rose of Texas Erotic Romance Author's and Publisher's Annual Convention. She called to let us know where she is so we won't worry about her. She wants to walk around over there for a bit. I didn't know it, but evidently, both Grace and Rachel have been doing some writing, and she wants to pick up literature and business cards for them and see if any of her favorite authors are over there signing autographs." Wes watched Evan's face closely as he added, "Rosemary also mentioned that a couple of the major e-publishers brought a bunch of their cover models with them, and they're wandering around the convention and posing for pictures with fans."

So predictable he was almost comical, Evan growled at the last comment. "I don't suppose she means the female models for the heroines?"

"Doubtful. I've gotten a look at some of the covers on her paperback collection. I think it's mostly 'man candy' over there. She said you would react like that and to tell you that there's not anyone over there that compares to either of us. I told her we would pick her up from there around noon. After lunch, she wants to spend the afternoon with you. She said she's looking forward to dressing up for us tonight, for the after-hours mixer."

"Good, I can't wait to see her in that sexy black dress she unpacked this morning. Thanks for letting me have a little time with her. I'm glad that she wants time alone with us."

"I can't wait, either. What are you going to do?"

"I'm gonna leave it up to her," Evan said with a little smile. Changing the subject before the growing bulge in his groin became more pronounced at the thought of being alone with Rosemary, Evan asked, "Did you see Ed and Cruz when they came by earlier?"

"Yeah, saw you talking to them. Wonder if Davina is wandering around here somewhere, too?"

"She'll probably put in an appearance at some point. I hope she keeps her hands to herself if Rosemary is around."

Wes chuckled. "Yeah, I can imagine the can of whoop-ass Rosemary would open up for her if she misbehaves."

* * * *

Rosemary looked around the crowded convention room at all the colorful booths and banners representing her favorite publishers and authors. Feeling like a little kid in a candy store, she waded into the enthusiastic chaos of talking people and twittering fans. Rosemary grinned as, here and there, she spotted more cover models, all dressed in costumes they must've worn for some of their cover shoots.

There were lots of cowboys, leather-clad biker dudes, as well as loin-cloth-clad otherworldly Lords and Explorers, along with the requisite vampires and were-shifters. Many were decorated with wild, sexy tattoos. There were also several that had military or mercenary looks to them.

They were all sexy as hell, but not one of them did anything for her. She still tingled pleasantly with the memory of her first ménage à trois from the night before. She planned to take plenty of pictures for the girls to enjoy, though.

Wandering around, she worked her way up one row then down the next. She stopped at the first e-publisher's booth she recognized the name of and mentioned both Grace and Rachel. The woman she spoke with briefly explained their submission process and gave Rosemary a business card and some printed literature to take to the girls and slipped a couple of complimentary new releases in the bag she handed to Rosemary, to thank her for stopping and asking.

A handsome and vaguely familiar cover model wandered over to that publisher's booth, and the woman enthusiastically took a picture of Rosemary with him, using Rosemary's cell phone camera. She recognized him as the cover model for one of her favorite erotic romances and asked him for his autograph, which he gladly signed for her. She moved on, and the process repeated itself twice more with other publishers and their cover models.

A man walked by, momentarily distracting her. Incongruous was the first word that came to Rosemary's mind. Not because of how he was dressed but because of his demeanor. She'd seen several models dressed as bad-ass biker dudes, all of them over six feet, tanned with sexy tattoos, dressed in leather or denim, looking sexy as hell, fresh from a cover shoot.

This guy was the real deal. His tats were genuine, not painted on, and fully sleeved both arms from the wrists up, disappearing beneath the rolled sleeves of his white T-shirt which were stretched tautly over his bulging biceps. The sexy hunk wore a black leather vest that was covered with patches and logos. On the back of the vest was the emblem embroidered for the motorcycle club he was a member of, along with what must be his nickname. "Bad Dog." He looked like a bad dog, too.

He walked over to one of the booths a few feet from where Rosemary stood surreptitiously watching him while she browsed through a book cover promo poster collection. She smiled, thinking that erotic romance *was* for everybody, not just women.

To each his own.

His tanned head was shaved smooth, and she noticed one of his tattoos peeked above the back of his T-shirt. He must've had a dragon tattoo on his back because to her it looked like the tail of a dragon snaking up and twining around to the base of his skull. He laughed at something the woman he was talking to said, and his voice had a rough, gravelly quality to it. Most of the cover models walking around averaged between six foot two and six foot five, but this guy topped out at five foot nine to five foot ten maximum. Mentally, she ticked through the list of authors she knew were here today and speculated on who he'd come to get an autograph from.

He finished his conversation, and she couldn't help but watch him as he walked by her. She wasn't interested in him so much as she was intrigued by him. His jeans were rumpled, and his boots were scuffed as he walked past her, holding her attention. He gave her a naughty, crooked grin and winked when she couldn't suppress a giggle and continued on his way.

She clicked a picture of him, for kicks, and went on her way, visiting with publishers, promoting Grace and Rachel and getting all kinds of information. Several of the publishers' representatives thought she was doing a really nice thing for her friends and slipped her extra copies of books and called cover models over to take pictures with her.

Over the PA system, an announcer promoted the beginning of a question and answer panel hosted by several authors. Evidently, many of the attendees were planning to participate. Rosemary would've gone, but her men would be picking her up soon, so she wandered the aisles as the crowds thinned considerably.

She was finishing a conversation with a new author promoting her first release from her publisher's booth when she looked up and noticed "Bad Dog" again. He was talking with an author as she sat at her booth, a stack of books at her left waiting to be signed. The banner behind her displayed the cover of her latest best-selling novel and her name in bold, brazen lettering, Tessa Malone.

The Tessa Malone! Rosemary felt a sincere fan-girl squeal coming on.

Ms. Malone looked like any other professional person present at the convention, maybe somebody's daughter or girlfriend, who also worked a full-time job. Her hair was styled and her nails manicured. She obviously took good care of herself but certainly did not look the celebrity type like Rosemary would've expected.

She'd read several of Ms. Malone's novels, having truly enjoyed her genius wit, clever, snappy dialogue, and larger-than-life characters. She specialized in over-the-top, alpha male heroes who took what they wanted and heroines who totally kicked ass, inspired adoring devotion in their alphas, and *swallowed* every time. Rosemary knew Rachel was a huge fan, as well.

Bad Dog stood talking privately to Ms. Malone at her table. Rosemary felt a little voyeuristic as she observed them. Bad Dog was momentarily distracted and looked away from her and down the aisle. Ms. Malone glanced at him with open adoration in her eyes, her cheeks blushing a soft rose color, before she looked down at her hands shyly.

Once again focused on her, Bad Dog surreptitiously stroked a finger over Tessa's knuckles. Tessa's lips popped open soundlessly, and she froze under his touch. The magnetism between them was palpable even from a distance. Rosemary wondered if she was watching a fledgling romance blossom before her eyes.

Tessa looked beyond him and made eye contact with Rosemary. *Oops! Busted!* Then the author glanced away just as quickly, looking up and smiling into Bad Dog's eyes. Bad Dog leaned down to her and whispered something to her before glancing behind him and then edged away, his finger once again stroking over the top of her hand.

Tessa closed her eyes and took a deep breath. Rosemary felt a little embarrassed for having stopped to witness that intimate exchange, but it wasn't like they'd made any attempt at being discreet. When she looked up at Rosemary, Tessa smiled at her and shrugged as if to say, "Men!"

Rosemary grinned back and made her way down to Tessa's table, drawn by curiosity and a genuine desire to meet her and get an autograph. Someone else approached Tessa first, and her attention was drawn to them. Tessa lifted a paperback and signed it then spoke a moment with them.

When Rosemary walked over, Tessa held her hands to her cheeks and whispered to her, "I think my cheeks are going to be sore from smiling so much. Hi, I'm Tessa Malone." She stuck her hand out to shake Rosemary's.

Rosemary shook her hand and said, "Sorry, I'm Rosemary Piper. I didn't mean to eavesdrop on your moment a bit ago. I find people watching very interesting and he seems so..."

"Out of place?" Tessa whispered and giggled when Rosemary nodded emphatically. "Oh, honey, you have *no* idea."

"Is he your boyfriend?" Rosemary asked conspiratorially. "Or is he a cover model? He looks like the real thing."

Tessa's sweet, hazel eyes sparkled as she laughed gaily. "Oh, he's no cover model, that's for sure. But he is a biker. He rode his Harley from the hotel this morning. He offered me a ride because I'm at the same hotel, but I wouldn't do it."

Rosemary's jaw dropped, and she looked in the direction Bad Dog had walked away. "Why not?"

"Well, I wasn't dressed for it but also because I didn't want to make a fool of myself. I'm a *bit* of a chicken. And no, he's not my boyfriend. He keeps doing things like that and..." Tessa blushed and sighed a little forlornly, looking in the direction he'd headed earlier, then looked away.

Tessa and Bad Dog looked like an unlikely pair, to be honest. She was dressed in a body-hugging black skirt and a silky red top and tall, black high-heeled boots. Tessa was curvaceous and reminded Rosemary somewhat of Grace, except that she had long, straight, dark brown hair and she wore rimless eyeglasses. However, opposites did attract.

Rosemary asked, "So is he a fan of yours?"

Tessa's eyes twinkled. "Well, I suppose, but if you keep wandering around, you'll probably see him again," Tessa said with a smile and a giggle then changed the subject, peeking in Rosemary's bag. "That's quite a collection of publisher's literature you have there. Are you a writer?"

"Me? No! But I have two dear friends who are. I'm here with my fiancés at the Home Builder's Convention on the other side of the Center, and I happened—"

"Wait." Tessa held up a hand then crooked her finger at Rosemary and giggled before whispering to her, "Your *what*? Did you say 'fiancés' as in *plural*?" Tessa drew out the last word into two long syllables and held up two fingers.

Rosemary giggled and felt her cheeks tingle with heat. Suddenly, *she* was the one under the microscope. Rosemary looked around before leaning in closer and nodded conspiratorially. "Uh-huh! That's *exactly* what I said. Wes and Evan." Their handsome faces flitted through her mind as well as glimpses of their explosive and beautiful lovemaking the night before. Her cheeks went red-hot at the reminder.

Tessa leaned forward eagerly, glancing around quickly. "What kind of work do they do?"

"Custom-made furniture. Bedroom furniture is their specialty. They built a big, custom bed for my friend and her three husbands," Rosemary said with another wicked giggle at Tessa's reaction. She looked about ready to jump out of her seat.

"*Holy shit!* The hell you say!"

"Yeah!"

"And you're *engaged* to two men? Where are you from, near here?" Tessa asked, sounding hopeful.

"We're all from Divine, a few hours northwest of here."

"I'd love to be able to talk to someone who actively, successfully lives that lifestyle. You don't know me at all, but would you mind if I contacted you online via e-mail sometime or on the phone? I promise I wouldn't stalk you or anything. I'd love to be able to do a little research. It would mean an awful lot to me."

"I'd be happy to talk to you and put you in touch with my friend. I can *guarantee* you she'd love to meet you," Rosemary said, taking a pen and small notepad from her purse and writing her e-mail address and phone number on it.

Tessa got a dreamy look in her eyes but straightened up as an elderly man came to her booth and said hello and then asked her to sign a copy of her book for his shy, little wife who hovered nearby. When the man departed, Tessa took a promo card from the stack in the middle of the table and wrote her e-mail address and Web site address on the back of it then handed her two more with the same information for Grace and Rachel.

Tessa whispered, "I live in Austin, but I'm this way all the time because I have family here. Maybe you'd like to get together for supper or lunch sometime. It would be a golden opportunity for me, and I'd be really grateful."

"Oh my gosh, they're gonna be so excited. They're both huge fans of yours!" Rosemary said, looking at what Tessa had written, realizing she'd written down a private e-mail address, as the e-mail address her fans could write to her at was already printed on the back of the card.

"We should take a picture for you to send to them. Gimme your camera phone. Max, come here for a second, would you?"

Rosemary looked up as Bad Dog made another sudden appearance. He grinned wickedly at Rosemary before turning his intense, dark gaze on Tessa.

"What is it, baby doll?" he asked in a rough, sexy voice.

Oh, mama, that voice! He called her baby doll.

The way he'd said it was equally as sexy, his intonation implying that he'd do *whatever* she wanted him to do.

"I want to take a picture with my new friend, Rosemary. She's going to help me with some research. Would you do the honors, please?"

"Sure, baby doll, anything for you." Bad Dog, also known as Max, took the camera from Rosemary and snapped several shots.

"You know, you should take a couple with Max, too, Rosemary. Tell your friends you got a picture with a real, bad-ass biker dude."

Max rolled his eyes, grinned, and handed Tessa the phone and murmured, "Sweet cheeks, you're getting my hopes up. I'm gonna get you on the back of my Harley one of these days."

Rosemary saw Tessa glance at him then look at the screen on the phone and murmured to him, "Someday, you never know. I might stop being such a chicken."

Rosemary giggled as Max put his arm around her shoulder and smiled while Tessa took the picture, and then she said, "My friend Grace always says, 'Seize the day and live life with no regrets.'"

Tessa giggled, blushing prettily, and said, "I'll bet she would know, too!"

"Yup." Turning to Max, Rosemary said, "Thank you for the pictures."

"Hey, no problem at all. Baby doll, if anybody asks, I'll be right back. I'm gonna get a bottle of water from the cooler. You need anything?"

"No, Max, but thanks for asking," Tessa replied, her eyes twinkling at him.

Max swaggered away, a crumpled red bandana hanging from his back pocket. Rosemary admired the tattoo at his neck and the ones on his arm again then turned back to Tessa. Tessa's eyes were a little glazed, and her cheeks were pink again as she watched him confidently saunter away, completely at ease through the mostly female crowd.

Rosemary snickered. "Wow, you are totally into him, aren't you?"

Never taking her eyes off of Max's ass until he disappeared from sight, Tessa murmured, "Oh, *yum*. Am I ever. But he lives in Houston and our schedules are crazy."

Rosemary crossed her arms in front of her and asked expectantly, like she was talking to an old friend, "Are you gonna take a ride with him tonight?"

Tessa looked up at her seriously, speculatively. "I should, shouldn't I? I have blue jeans in my suitcase, and I could tie back my hair. But I'm kind of intimidated by his Harley. What if I'm…" She paused, pointing at her curvaceous backside.

Rosemary couldn't suppress the naughty little grin that spread across her face as she said, "Tessa, if he *wants* you on the back of his Harley, you can bet that he can *handle* you being back there. Seems to me like he kind of likes…" Rosemary mirrored Tessa, trailing off and pointed at her own backside.

Tessa blushed and giggled again. "You're right. I think I might do it."

A whole horde of adoring fans discovered Tessa's table, and Rosemary winked at her and whispered, "*Go for it*," then waved. "We'll be in touch with you."

Rosemary walked around a while longer. Meeting Tessa and Max was definitely the highlight of the morning spent at the convention, or so she *thought.*

She was snapping pictures of a group of cover models who were all hamming it up and posing together when her eye was drawn by a glimpse of a red bandana. She realized it was Max then looked back to the group of models to take another picture and did a double take.

Max had walked over to a table positioned about half a row down from Tessa's and then moved behind it and sat down. Rosemary's mouth fell open in shock when she took in the banner on the front of his table. On the wall behind Max hung a full-color reproduction of the cover art for the latest bestseller, written by one of the biggest selling, most popular authors in the erotic romance genre.

A woman walked up to Max and shook his hand. He spoke briefly, smiling at her, then removed a paperback from a box under the table and autographed it for her. The woman thanked him profusely then stumbled away in awe, showing her giggling friends his autograph. He caught Rosemary staring open-mouthed at him and chuckled, giving her a crooked little grin.

She walked over to his booth. "*You're* Lorelei DeVeaux?" she asked, her hand on her hip.

"Een zee flesh!" he said, grinning as she laughed. "So what did Tessa say about me? Isn't she something?"

"She sure is. So, 'Bad Dog' lives a double life as best-selling author Lorelei DeVeaux. I had no idea. I guess I don't get out enough. I *love* your books."

Max pulled some from a box, signed them, and gave them to her as he said, "Here's one for you and for your two girl friends." Rosemary thanked him and he asked cheekily, "So did you tell Tessa what a nice guy you think I am and how it's so obvious I adore her?"

"Well, your name did come up in the conversation, but I can't tell you what was said. *I* think you should ask her *again* to take a ride with you tonight. She might change her mind. You never know. So, you live in Houston?"

"For now, but I'm moving soon."

"Oh, really? Why?"

Max looked around to see if anyone listened to them. "Well, I can write from anywhere, and Tessa doesn't believe in long-distance relationships. I own property outside of Austin, and I've always planned on building a house there. I figured I'd go ahead and get started on it, maybe start building a life to go along with it."

Rosemary nodded in approval. "Two best-selling erotic romance authors in a relationship together, wow…"

"Setting the sheets *aflame*," Max whispered melodramatically with a smirk, "She'd reduce me to ashes with that brilliant, sexy mind of hers."

Rosemary's mouth popped open. "Oh, you're good!"

Max looked over her shoulder, his eyebrow raised, and a knowing smile lit his face. "No, I think *you're* good," he said speculatively, grinning as his suspicion was confirmed.

She jumped when she felt warm hands slide down her forearms and rough, calloused fingers entwine with hers.

"Hey, Rosemary," Evan murmured in her ear, nodding at Max.

"Hi, baby," Wes whispered. "We've come to collect you for lunch. From the looks of things in here, you've been having a good time."

Allowing them to pull her to them for a kiss one at a time, Rosemary nodded and said, "It's been a lot of fun! I met all kinds of publishers for the girls and some of my favorite authors. Speaking of which, I'd like you to meet Lorelei DeVeaux." She giggled as she indicated her new friend. "This is Max. DeVeaux is his pen name."

"Really? Pleased to meet you, man," Evan said as he held out a hand to shake with Max. "I think we need to thank you for secondary benefits. Your book is on her bedside table at home."

Max laughed good-naturedly with them. "Max Stone. Hey, you're welcome, man. Glad to be of service. So, you're...?" Max asked curiously, looking for some sort of confirmation, winking at Rosemary.

"Max, these are my fiancés, Wes and Evan Garner," Rosemary said, lifting a hand to each of them respectively. "They're taking me to lunch."

A wide grin appeared on Max's face. "Wow. Seriously?"

"Rosemary, do you think that's a good idea?" Evan said, glancing at Wes.

"Honey, if there was any place in the universe where I wouldn't worry about judgment over our relationship, it is surely within these walls. You should read some of Lorelei's hot ménage love scenes," Rosemary said, giggling as she slid her arms possessively around their waists. "I brought that one from home with me this weekend. Maybe we need a bedtime story tonight." A thrill went up her spine when she heard their faint growls.

Max pulled out a promo card with the cover of the new book on one side and his e-mail and Web site address on the other, wrote on it, and handed it to Wes. "It's a pleasure to meet the two of you. If you'd be interested, I'd like to chat with you sometime, purely in a research sense about your relationship dynamic."

Wes glanced at Evan, who shrugged but didn't look put off by the idea, and nodded. "Sure, we'll get in touch sometime. Good luck with your writing. It's nice to meet you, Max."

"Same here. It's nice to meet you, Rosemary. And thanks for the good word you put in for me with Tessa. So you think she'd take a ride with me tonight?"

Rosemary grinned at him and said, "Bad Dog, I'd bet money on it. Good luck, I think she's quite a catch. Does she know you're planning a move to Austin?"

"Naw, not yet. I don't want her to feel pressured."

"I think knowing you'll be closer might encourage her. Tessa's beautiful and kind, too."

"Isn't she, though? Thanks, Rosemary. Enjoy your lunch." A few seconds later, the same group of giggling fans that had descended on Tessa earlier discovered Max, and Rosemary said good-bye.

"You mean he's not gay?" Wes whispered in her ear as they walked away, their arms still wrapped around her. She shook her head as she glanced back at Max and winked. Several of the girls were gawking at the three of them.

Rosemary overheard one of the girls ask Max, "Are those three cover models from one of your ménage romances? They're really *hot*!"

Chapter Fourteen

Evan had given Rosemary the choice to return to the bed and breakfast for a little down time, take a riverboat ride on the San Antonio River, or visit the Rivercenter Mall. Rosemary had opted to make the short trip back to the bed and breakfast. A choice Evan's eager, hardening cock was all on board with.

Evan and Rosemary received another dirty, disapproving look from the same woman they'd encountered the night before in the dining room as they quietly made their way upstairs. This time a friend sat with her and they both glared at Rosemary with censure in their eyes.

"Were we too noisy last night?" Rosemary whispered to Evan as they topped the first landing.

"Nobody complained to either me or Wes." Evan squeezed her hand. "Her imagination has probably run wild, and she thinks we'll be up there swinging from the light fixtures or something. Try to ignore her." He and Wes had made reservations to take Rosemary out to a nice restaurant later that night. He counted it a bonus that they wouldn't have to see that woman downstairs in the dining room again. Rosemary giggled and shrugged. Maybe she hadn't noticed the way he shielded her from the view of the two unfriendly women as they'd turned to gossip with each other as he'd led her up the stairs.

His goal right now was to be alone with Rosemary and relax together for a few hours. Once in the room, she turned to Evan with a beautiful smile and stripped. He'd planned to take it slow, but she was naked inside twenty seconds.

"Baby, how are you, after last night, I mean?" Evan asked, his cock screaming in protest for him to shut up and get on board with *Rosemary's* plan.

The sight of Rosemary, naked and wanting him, still stole his breath from him. "I'm going to need a few days rest before we try anal or a ménage again, but otherwise, I'm fine. My body tingles anytime I get near the two of you because I want more."

Behind his fly, his cock bobbed and twitched, ready to be of service. "Well, you can have *more*, but I'm letting you set the pace, okay? We even have time for a nap, later."

"That sounds perfect. I'm happy I get to spend some time alone with you today. I figured you wouldn't mind missing out on shopping at the mall." She giggled as he rolled his eyes, knowing that he'd rather take a poke in the eye with a sharp stick than go to a mall.

Evan sat down on the edge of the bed and drew her to him, nuzzling her fragrant cleavage as he wrapped his hands around her curvy hips and squeezed her to him. He breathed in her mouth-watering, womanly fragrance and smiled as he remembered waking up with her sprawled limp over him that morning.

Her torso had been half draped over his as if he'd pulled her over him when he'd rolled to his back in his sleep. Her head rested on his other shoulder and her cheek, chest, and breasts were plastered to him.

Her flesh was warm and tender from being under the cozy covers. He'd buried his nose at her throat and lay there breathing in her tantalizing scent, slightly floral-like soap mixed with her natural essence. That was how he looked forward to waking up each morning very soon, the scent of her surrounding him, breathing her in and out.

"I love the way you smell, Rosemary. So sexy. Like my woman."

Rosemary sighed and sounded happy as she slid her fingers into his hair, massaging the muscles in his neck and then lightly grazing her fingernails down his back, giving him shivers. He released her, unbuttoned his shirt and let her slide it from his shoulders. Boots, jeans, and boxers followed then he backed up to the pillows at the head of the bed, bringing her with him. Crawling into his lap, she straddled him and pressed him to lie down.

Thunder rumbled distantly, and he was vaguely aware of the sound of raindrops splattering heavily against the window glass. The room was cool and dim, and the sound of the rain contributed to the languorous mood of the afternoon that lay before them. He wanted to savor each moment alone with her.

Rolling onto his side with her, Evan drew her lush body to his and suckled her nipples in complete quiet contentment as his arousal for her grew. He swept his hand from her neck, down her spine, and to her ass then lifted a thigh and drew it to him, fitting her more intimately to his body. He sought out her full lips with his own and relished her kiss, smiling when she playfully teased him with the tip of her tongue at his lower lip before pulling her closer to kiss her more intensely.

Rosemary's long, curly hair fell to his chest and shoulders, and her intoxicating scent invaded his nostrils again. She straddled his thighs, brushing her hard nipples over his chest as she relaxed against him. His hands stroked slowly over her satiny smooth back, back and forth, enjoying the feel of her skin and the sweet, solid presence of her lying on him like this.

Evan allowed his hands to stray farther south to her ass and massage the smooth twin globes, squeezing and stroking, feeling her skin grow warmer under his touch. Her thighs were relaxed on either side of his. He skimmed his hands down the backs of her thighs, stroking up and down repeatedly before sliding farther up to her pussy.

Her head fell to his chest limply, and she hissed as his fingertips stroked over her damp outer lips, seeking entrance to the slick, pooled moisture that lay within. He slid a fingertip through her liquid, hot slit, searching for and finding her clit. His cock was an aching, twitching pole demanding entrance into her wet heat, but he refused to rush. The damned bastard could wait a little while at least.

He smiled when she moaned again, and her hips flexed against his questing fingers. Raising her head, she looked into his eyes and leaned in to kiss him. With her lips on his, the love in her eyes, and her little body perched on him like this, his little Rosemary was everything to him. Her inky black curls fell around them as their lips met again. He released her pussy and wrapped his arms around her, one hand tenderly gripping her ass and the other holding her shoulder, as he groaned with the depth of what he was feeling.

He looked into her violet eyes and whispered over the lump in his throat, "Rosemary, I love you." He rolled her to her back and thrust his cock into her seeping pussy, straight to the hilt in one smooth, sliding stroke. Her breath tickled his ear as it came in velvety, rasping pants, music to his ears.

"I love the sounds you make when we make love to you. Even the way you breathe is sexy to me. Did you know that?"

"Yes. Tell me more. I love it when you tell me what you like," she murmured, flicking his throat with her tongue before sucking on it.

"I love the way your breathing changes to that high-pitched, soft panting right before you come. Gets me even harder if that's possible."

"Oh yeah? Tell me more."

"I love the way you tilt your head and arch your back and the way you sometimes go still and quiet right before you come really hard. I love to feel your claws on my back and dug into my ass when we're fucking hard and fast. And I love having you all to myself right now, with just the two of us. I almost feel guilty I love it so much."

"Don't," she whispered as she wrapped her arms around his neck and undulated against him. "We're going to regularly spend time alone with each other. I need this time with you, Evan. Just like I'll need it with Wes. I love being with you both, but I also need to give you my undivided attention."

He thrust against her, taking his time, whispering more love words and stroking them both into white-hot ecstasy. She seemed to draw something beneficial from this time besides satisfying sex. Once they were finished, he rolled onto his back again, never losing their intimate connection, his cock still buried inside her. Rosemary shivered lightly as she drifted toward sleep, and he pulled the top sheet and blanket over them so she wouldn't get chilled.

The rain continued to fall outside the window, lightning flickering followed by the distant swell of thunder. They talked for a while, his hands sweeping over her back, pushing her knees down so that their legs were entwined together and she could be more comfortable. He stroked her shoulders and her arms, watching the sweep of her thick, black lashes as she blinked before her eyes finally drifted closed.

Evan lay there for a while, his hands drifting over her hips. He loved the feel of her curvaceous body snuggled against him, his cock still engulfed within her. A prideful, possessive feeling roared inside him.

He wanted to be what she needed, to provide her with what she wanted, and to honor the trust she felt in him. This is what Jack and the guys told him and Wes it would feel like. Jealousy would be put aside when he knew, without a doubt, that her needs, her love, and her happiness came first.

Evan remembered what Grace had told him the first time he'd talked alone with her. Some women weren't *just* good. They were *damn* good. Like Jack and the others, Wes and Evan had found a woman who was worthy of that title.

Evan woke some time later to the sound of angry voices in the hallway. He held Rosemary to him as she startled awake, shushing and calming her. They listened to the voices out in the hallway, muted female voices and what he now recognized as Wes's angry tone.

The door never rattled or opened, and the voices subsided as the angry conversation was evidently taken downstairs. Evan was still groggy and thought for several moments about drifting back to sleep and letting Wes deal with whatever disturbance had occurred. But the more his mind focused, the more awake he became. Had somebody been outside the door when Wes arrived?

"What do you suppose that was all about?" Rosemary asked in a sleepy, slurred voice. He glanced at the bedside clock and kissed her forehead.

"You've only been asleep for half an hour, Rosemary. Why don't you rest some more? I'll go find out." They both groaned when she shifted on him, and his softened cock slid from her warm, wet depths. This was *not* how he'd envisioned waking from their nap. She murmured something unintelligible as she curled up like a kitten on his pillow and fell back asleep.

He rose from the bed and slipped into his clothing from earlier, put his shoes on, and then silently let himself out of the room after glancing back at her lush, sleeping form nestled in the bedclothes. He went downstairs quietly, following the sounds of an angry conversation in the front hall.

The owner and manager of The Crystal Rose Bed and Breakfast, Bill Farmer, was standing at the front desk with a police officer, Wes, and, no big surprise there, the disapproving woman and her friend. The police officer was looking decidedly perturbed at the two women, who were both talking non-stop, pointing their fingers at him, at Wes, and at the ceiling. Finally, the police officer raised his hands and got them all to quiet down as Evan joined the group, which was being watched avidly by others in the living room and parlor of the bed and breakfast.

"Mr. Farmer, is there perhaps a more private place to take this discussion?" the police officer asked discreetly.

"Sure, follow me," Mr. Farmer said as he indicated a back hallway that led to the kitchen. Clearing out the staff, they all stood around the center island while the police officer consulted his notepad and spoke succinctly into his radio before turning it down a little.

"All right. You, sir. Tell me what you saw?" the police officer asked, indicating Wes. The officer turned intimidating eyes on the woman, who had opened her mouth. When she stilled and closed her mouth, he looked back to Wes.

"I returned from the Convention Center fifteen minutes ago, made my way to the third floor where our suite is located, and found these women on their knees in front of my door, taking turns peeking in the keyhole," Wes said angrily as Evan gritted his teeth in outrage beside him.

The police officer rolled his eyes heavenward. "Ma'am, I'm afraid to ask, but why were you peeking in their keyhole?"

"We—we heard noises from downstairs. They make a lot of noise, Officer. It's shameful! *Just shameful!* These two men are sharing a woman here this weekend. They're all in the same room! They keep us *awake* at night!"

Mr. Farmer interjected, "Now, Mrs. Breck. You and I both know there is *no way* they could be disturbing you. You're on the first floor at the opposite end of the house."

The woman puffed herself up self-righteously and said, "Nevertheless, we heard noises, and we went to investigate. What they do up there is immoral and also *illegal*. You should arrest these men, Officer! And that slut they parade around with."

Evan clenched his fists, tempted for the first time to use them to shut this bitch up.

"Now wait a damned minute—" Wes began, outraged.

"What noises did you hear?" the officer asked Mrs. Breck, holding his hand up for silence from everyone else.

Mrs. Breck looked scandalized, so her friend blushingly provided the answer in a shocked stage whisper. *"Sex noises, officer."*

The innkeeper threw his hands up in the air. "Heaven forbid someone should be having sex under my roof," Mr. Farmer muttered sarcastically. "Mrs. Breck, my brochure clearly states that visitors to our bed and breakfast can expect to enjoy a relaxing, *romantic* atmosphere. Romance generally leads to sex, for *some* people. They're staying in the *Bridal* Suite, which is all by itself on the top floor. There is no way you could've heard sex noises, unless *you* were on the top floor."

The police officer turned to Evan. "Son, who might you be, and what is your business here?"

Evan leaned a hip against the center island. "Evan Garner, sir. Until the moment I was awakened by a disturbance outside my bedroom door, I was asleep in the Bridal Suite."

"Oh! But you weren't alone!" Mrs. Breck's friend squawked accusingly.

Evenly, he made his reply. "No, ma'am, I wasn't. Not that it's any of your business."

The officer consulted his notebook. "How long had you been in the room, and how long were you asleep?"

"We returned to our room after lunch, around one thirty. We were only asleep for about half an hour, so we must've fallen asleep around three o'clock. We noticed these women downstairs in the lobby when we arrived, looking down their noses at us. We do not parade around, as they say. We were barely holding hands. Because of their unfriendly demeanors, we don't spend any time in the lobby or common rooms, even though we have the right. We sat through our dinner last night while you bored holes with your eyes into Miss Piper the whole time."

Mrs. Breck demanded stridently, "Officer, I demand you arrest these two men! They're *both* having sex with that decadent whore upstairs!" Her face flushed a brilliant crimson to accompany her melodramatic words.

"And how do you know that, ma'am?" the police officer said, drilling her with his steely eyes.

"I saw them! They both have sex with her!" Then she covered her mouth with her hand. In the heat of the moment, she'd given herself away. Her friend looked guilty as hell, too.

Turning to Wes, the officer asked, "Mr. Garner, at what time did you discover these two peeking in your keyhole?"

"Around three twenty. On their knees, both of them, at the door."

"I'll be right back," the police officer murmured as he left them in silence. While he was gone, Rosemary joined their tense little group in the kitchen. Wes and Evan took her aside and quietly explained to her what was happening.

The police officer returned a minute later, his rain slicker dripping. He noted the presence of sleepy-eyed Rosemary with a nod, surmising who she was. "The drapes and blinds on the third floor are all closed. Looking at the house from the yard and from the sidewalk, even with the blinds, drapes, and curtains opened, nothing could be seen from ground level, and the trees are too thick around the house for any neighbors to see in the third-story windows. Mr. Farmer, has anyone else complained this weekend about noises coming from the third floor?"

Mr. Farmer shook his head negatively. "None. Both of the two rooms directly below theirs are currently rented, and neither guest has voiced any objection at all."

The police officer turned back to Mrs. Breck and drilled her with an intense stare. "Exactly how would you know that this woman was having sex with both of these men, unless you had been at their keyhole more than once?"

Mrs. Breck's fleshy jowls wobbled and flapped uselessly as she repeatedly opened and closed her mouth. Finally, she slammed her lips closed. The police officer raised an eyebrow at her then turned to Wes and Evan and flashed a conciliatory smile at Rosemary. "Do you wish to press charges for voyeurism?"

Mrs. Breck sputtered in outrage. "Officer, what you should be doing is arresting these three on charges of lewd conduct! It is illegal for them to be doing what they're doing! This is outrageous! *We* called you to deal with *them!*" she shouted, waving her bony finger at their little group.

"Lady, in your day it may have been illegal, but times have changed and the law books along with them. I don't care if they've got six people in that room, much less three. As long as they aren't disturbing the peace and are confining their romance to the bedroom, I'm not going to interfere. You, however, are on thin ice. What you just confessed to doing *is illegal* and *definitely* disturbing the peace."

Mrs. Breck and her friend stood in stunned silence. Wes and Evan looked at Rosemary, who looked at Mr. Farmer. Common sense told Evan that poor Mr. Farmer would really love to avoid explaining to his other guests why two of his guests were being carted away in handcuffs. That sort of thing was not good for business. He probably liked the outstanding reviews he received online and wouldn't want to see that image tarnished.

Mr. Farmer smiled in relief, obviously catching the ball when Rosemary threw it into his court. Rosemary turned to the police officer and replied, "I don't think any real damage was done, nothing that makes it worth the damage Mr. Farmer is risking by having two relatively normal-looking women carted away in a squad car. We have an important formal function to get ready for, and I don't think it's worth the headache to press charges, if they vacated the premises immediately. By the way, who contacted the police department?"

The police officer made notes on his pad and jerked a thumb back at the two women. "They did. Over an hour ago. I've been busy with a car accident, or I'd have been here sooner. If they were up there and hearing sex noises, that means they were outside your door for over an hour, plus whatever time they were up there prior to today. Are you sure you don't want to press charges? Mr. Farmer?"

Rosemary snorted in derision as she looked both women over and finally said, "And they say we're the perverts?"

Mrs. Breck's face turned a darker shade of magenta, and she looked about ready to blow a gasket.

Mr. Farmer offered his solution. "Officer, if it's all right, I plan to eject both these ladies within the next half hour. I hope that will be the extent of it. And Anastacia Breck and Marjorie Horton, *just you wait* until I call your husbands and tell them what you've been up to. You'll never hear the end of this!" he added in outrage as he pointed to the hallway.

Before they turned to go, Mrs. Breck couldn't resist a parting shot. "Decadent whore. You're up there fornicating with two men. You should be *ashamed*!"

As Evan and Wes scowled at the woman, Rosemary smiled with saccharine sweetness and said, "Peeping Tom. You're staying in a room with another woman in a romantic bed and breakfast. Does that mean you two are lesbians?" If they had been, Evan knew Rosemary wouldn't have said a single word to either of them about it or singled them out in any way.

The police officer held up a hand when Mrs. Breck would've responded and said, "Lady, you'd better cut your losses before I call a judge and ask if I can still bring you two in since I got a clear confession from you. We don't take kindly to degenerates peeping into people's private hotel rooms in a tourist town." He turned to Wes, Evan, and Rosemary. "Sorry, folks, for all the inconvenience. I hope the rest of your stay in our city is much friendlier." He put his plastic-covered cowboy hat back on his head and stuck his notepad back in his pocket.

Mr. Farmer turned to them briefly, promising to make it up to them before escorting Mrs. Breck and Mrs. Horton to their rooms to collect their belongings and give them the boot. They returned to the third floor as the kitchen staff re-entered the kitchen and jumped into a flurry of activity.

"I think I'm going to take a nice, long, hot bath," Rosemary said quietly as she sifted through the contents of her suitcase, looking for fresh undergarments, then collected her robe.

Evan and Wes followed her into the spacious bathroom, and Wes spoke up. "Baby, are you all right?"

Rosemary chuckled a little as she shook her head. "I feel violated because they must've had their eyes to the keyhole more than once this weekend. At least it wasn't a sex pervert peeping in on us, just two bitter, dried-up, self-righteous old hags who probably haven't had sex since the seventies. Grace warned me about women like them. I've dealt with others in Divine who are every bit as bad. I feel tense right now, but a nice, hot bath should do the trick."

A knock sounded at the door, and Evan welcomed Mr. Farmer in from where he and his wife stood in embarrassment on the threshold. Mr. Farmer apologized to all three of them again and told them that the women were already gone.

Mrs. Farmer explained that they'd been reluctant to update the old-fashioned doorknobs with brand-new ones, wanting to keep the look of their establishment authentic. After today's incident, they had decided to contact a locksmith and update the doors to every guest room so this could never happen again. Before they departed, Mr. Farmer told them that a complimentary bottle of champagne would be waiting for them upon their return to their room that evening.

Rosemary dimmed the lights and lit candles then soaked luxuriously in her fragrant bubbles. Evan and Wes joined her in the huge bath tub, with plenty of time on their hands and her in their arms. Rosemary told him and Wes that they truly did make her feel decadent, in the very best sense of the word.

Chapter Fifteen

Dressed in a dark business suit, Evan waited with Wes in the hallway off of the bed-and-breakfast's living room for Rosemary to come downstairs. She'd told them she wanted to surprise them, making an entrance on the stairs. From where he now stood, Evan could hear the faint clicking of her high heels on the second-story landing. Other guests sat in the parlor and living room, waiting until dinner was served and were *all eyes* as the men waited expectantly.

The first thing he saw were her pretty, little, black peep-toed pumps and her slim ankles beneath the long hemline of her sexy, black evening gown. The gown flowed with her movements as she descended the stairs, the flowing drape in the front revealing a slit that reached above her knee. The gown draped attractively over her breasts and revealed just enough of her silky cleavage.

Before leaving the room when she was about to dress, Wes had removed the rectangular velvet box from his luggage. He and Evan presented her with a string of pearls and pearl earrings. Evan had been afraid for a few minutes that she would cry because her voice had trembled as she thanked them and her eyes had been teary, but she'd told them she'd pull it together and be down in a few minutes.

The choker fit her slim neck perfectly and looked gorgeous. The only other jewelry she wore was her gold engagement ring. She was so beautiful she made his heart pound with love. His greedy cock throbbed in echoing agreement.

Evan heard a movement from the living room and looked over, realizing everyone in the place was watching her come down the stairs, some of them even coming to stand in the hallway. Evan watched Rosemary as she took the last few steps down, and she smiled and blushed when she met the other guests' gazes. Several of them nodded at her and she smiled back, but Evan could see the hint of apprehension in her eyes. Would anybody else say rude things to her? If they didn't want a broken jaw, they'd better keep their holier-than-thou thoughts to themselves.

Neither Evan nor his brother had planned on having an audience for this moment as they helped her arrange her wrap on her shoulders, over the backless gown, but the onlookers seemed more curiously friendly than judgmental. Evan supposed many of them had to have heard at least part of the confrontation earlier and had possibly even heard the two women at their gossip that weekend in the common rooms.

An elderly lady approached them and patted Rosemary's arm and said, "Dear, you look *just* lovely. I hope you have a wonderful time tonight." Then she and her husband led the others away as the dinner chime rang.

Evan chuckled. "Saved by the bell."

Wes offered Rosemary his arm. "Ready to have a night on the town with your men, baby?"

"Yes, I am."

* * * *

After eating dinner at an exclusive restaurant on the Riverwalk, Wes, Rosemary, and Evan returned to the Convention Center where the after-hours mixer was being held. Wes pulled open one of the numerous glass doors to allow Rosemary to precede them into the building. The floor vibrated under Wes's feet with a heavy bass beat.

Rosemary turned to him with curiosity in her eyes. "This isn't prom season, is it?"

Wes raised an eyebrow at Evan. "I don't think so. That's usually in the spring, isn't it? *Where* is that music coming from?" As they made their way across the massive foyer in the direction of the Home Builder's Association mixer, Wes noticed the sound faded.

Rosemary turned to them, laughing, her eyes dancing with merriment. "That music is coming from the Rose of Texas Convention. They must be having a dance. Oh, I bet *they're* having a good time!"

Wes smiled at her and said, "Well, if it's boring at our mixer, we can always crash their dance, huh?"

Rosemary nodded her head, looking all on board with that idea. "You wouldn't have to twist my arm. I wonder if Max got Tessa to agree to go on that moonlight motorcycle ride with him."

They approached the entry doors to their meeting room and ushered her in. Most of the attendees were dressed up for the affair, drinks in hand, wandering around chatting with their fellow professionals. Another room had been opened up, adjacent to the exhibit area where many people still wandered and chatted, and a band was set up on a stage playing while a few couples danced.

Evan and Wes escorted her to the bar and got drinks, and then they wandered around for a bit, introducing her to several of their acquaintances. She made small talk with everyone, not hanging back a bit, clearly in her element. No one seemed to bat an eyelash at her presence there with both Wes and Evan, even though they weren't that careful about which of them put an arm around her waist or her shoulders, and it was the same for her. When Wes had asked her at supper about it, she told them she preferred to play it by ear. She'd told him that after the drama earlier in the day, anyone who objected could kiss her lily-white ass. Typical, sassy Rosemary. The feisty one's reappearance had made Wes laugh out loud.

Rosemary was equally hands on with both of them, though not in an overt way. She might be feeling brave, but Wes knew she wouldn't do anything to provoke comment. Anyone watching her would've noted that at times she held hands with Wes then at other times held hands with Evan.

When asked about her engagement ring, she replied that she and Wes were going to be married in the spring sometime and left it at that. She always managed to steer the conversation away from wedding plans and put the spotlight on others before they had a chance to ask any more questions.

The three of them still planned to elope, so there were no wedding plans to talk about. Just a beach, a preacher, the love of his life, his brother, and a ring.

* * * *

After chatting with friends and networking for an hour, Rosemary was ready to take a turn on the dance floor. More attendees had arrived by this point, and the dance floor was full when Wes held out his hand. The band was done for the evening, and a DJ was now playing a selection of dance music. Her ears perked up when the telltale waltzing lilt of "Strawberry Wine" by Deana Carter began to play.

Wes smiled knowingly at her. "Dance with me, baby? I hear a waltz."

Rosemary beamed at him. "I'd love to." She slipped into his arms, winking at Evan as he took a seat at their table. She snuggled close to Wes like she'd been dancing with him all her life, which technically she *had*. They'd learned how to dance together with Evan and several other friends, including Rachel. Wes's warm hand felt good pressed to her lower back, the other cupping her hand. Being held like this made her feel precious to him.

She looked into Wes's eyes admiringly. Both of them were so handsome in their dark suits, black cowboy boots, and felt cowboy hats.

"You look beautiful tonight, Rosemary," Wes whispered to her, pressing a kiss to her temple.

"Thank you. You're pretty handsome yourself, Wes." She pressed closer, breathing in his clean, manly scent. Rosemary loved the way both her men smelled, though they were totally different. Wes always smelled good like soap and fresh air and woodsy sometimes if she caught him after he'd been in the woodshop. Evan was similar in that respect, but his unique scent was more spicy and outdoorsy. They were both mouthwatering to be with.

After taking several more circuits on the dance floor, Wes led her back to their table as the song ended. Rosemary felt the mouthy bitch in her rear up and try to take control.

Gritting her teeth, she took in the sight before her. A well-built blonde had pressed herself flat against Evan and had her arms draped over his shoulders. Rosemary noted that Evan didn't look pleased with the attention at all. The blonde had him backed up against their table, and he was seeking an exit, judging by his body language. The bitch slid her hands inside Evan's jacket as she pressed against him, and Rosemary felt her ears grow hot.

I'm about to whip somebody's ass.

"Who in the hell is that?" Rosemary asked, not even trying to hide the bite in her tone. Wes stiffened at her side and cleared his throat.

"Easy, baby. Her name is Davina Morley. Up until a few months ago, she was our account rep from Papillion Paint and Finish."

She thought she'd recognized the woman who had visited the shop a couple of months before but hadn't gotten a good enough look at her to be sure. Davina took her life into her hands as she slowly and suggestively rubbed her ample breasts against Evan's chest. Wes caressed Rosemary's waist soothingly as she walked beside him.

"She takes the idea of *servicing* an account to a different level," Rosemary muttered as they approached the table.

Davina evidently already had a couple of drinks in her. She was draped like an octopus on Evan, with more hands than he seemed like he knew what to do with. Judging by his sudden, jerking reaction, she'd just grabbed his ass.

Definitely about to whip somebody's ass.

Wes paused in his stride and turned to her, drawing her attention to him. He rubbed her shoulders, and she realized how tense she suddenly was. "Why don't you ask Evan to dance and let me deal with her?"

Rosemary curled her lip in disgust and glanced at Davina again. "I'll bet she's bathed in perfume, and now it's all over his jacket. If I go dance with Evan, then she'll be all over you, too."

Wes touched her chin with a gentle fingertip. "No, baby. You go rescue him, and while you're gone, I'll remind Davina about a little talk we had with her about stuff like this. That's why she's not our account rep anymore."

"Oh," Rosemary said with what she hoped was convincing innocence. She already knew that. She'd heard that particular conversation practically word for word. It was the only reason she didn't have Davina by the hair down on the floor.

Davina was tugging on Evan's jacket lapels, attempting to get him out on the dance floor. He was trying to be nice about it as he refused her, but it was obvious his good nature was wearing thin.

When Rosemary and Wes reached the table, she noticed that they were indeed enveloped in a cloud of cloying perfume. She wrinkled her nose, but smiled at Evan as Wes released her hand.

Smiling lovingly at Evan so he would know she wasn't upset with him, Rosemary ignored Davina entirely and said, "Evan, I'm ready for our dance now."

Davina turned to her and squinted at her. "Who are you?"

Opting for simple, Rosemary replied, "I'm Evan's."

"Evan's what?"

"*Just* Evan's. Would you mind removing your hands from his jacket?"

Surprised, Davina complied. "What do you mean you're *Evan's*?"

"I'm here with Evan," Rosemary explained, feeling like she was talking to a four year old.

Davina shrugged and reached for Wes with a leer. "That's okay. Come on, Wes, honey. Let's go shake it."

Resisting the urge to bar the woman's grasp of Wes and place a well-aimed fist in Davina's face, Rosemary helped Evan slip out of his jacket and left it hanging over the chair back. Davina already had her hands all over Wes, to Rosemary's disgust.

Wes carefully grasped Davina's hands and removed them from his shirtfront. "No, Davina, I can't."

"Why not?" Dang, she was persistent, or really drunk.

"I'm here with Rosemary."

Davina squinted owlishly at the three of them in confusion. She lifted her mixed drink unsteadily to her lips then said, "Well now, wait a minute. If she's Evan's and he's hers and you're here with Rosemary, then…who am I gonna dance with?" she asked in a whiny voice. The pouty lip was not a good look for her.

Rosemary glanced up at Evan, and he rolled his eyes in disgust.

Removing her persistent hands again, Wes replied, "Sorry, Davina. It'll have to be with somebody else. We told you once before we're in a relationship. We're not gonna hurt Rosemary's feelings by dancing with anyone else. Why don't you go dance with Ed?"

Evan whispered to Rosemary, "Ed's wife will have his head if he does." Rosemary giggled and allowed him to lead her to the dance floor.

Rosemary smirked. She wouldn't mind if the guys danced with others, but octopus arms didn't need to know that.

"She's a piece of work."

"You have no idea."

Oh, yeah, I do. 'Cause I'm a big, fat eavesdropper. She still felt a little guilty for doing that.

"I noticed Davina's got busy hands, too. She was groping you pretty good."

Evan snorted in disgust. "The only one I want groping me is you, baby. Are you having fun?"

"Mmm-hmm," she replied tensely as she watched Davina persist in trying to talk Wes into giving her a dance. Rosemary gave Wes a lot of credit for trying, but Davina wasn't taking the polite hint. She was probably too inebriated for that.

"I'll bet you'd like to put in an appearance at that other convention's party, wouldn't you?" Evan asked intuitively.

Rosemary grinned crookedly. "Like you read about, baby!" She was in the mood to have a good time with her men and was ready to do more than dance to waltzes and make polite small talk. She needed to let her hair down a bit.

"Davina is persisting, and this party is starting to die down. Why don't we rescue Wes and see about getting into that dance party at the other convention?"

"I love the way you think, Evan. You're my hero."

* * * *

Evan leaned down and kissed Rosemary on his way out the back door. Her lower lip tingled where he'd flicked it playfully with his tongue, making her want to stop him and claim another, more thorough kiss from him.

He looked back at her through the screen door as he closed it behind him and grinned.

Big tease.

Grace smiled knowingly and sighed. "Those two sure do look like your little trip last weekend agreed with them. I never knew Evan had dimples."

"Yeah, he's been smiling a lot more lately," Rosemary said, watching the man in question through the screen door that led out to the back deck where all the men were milling around the grill, relaxing with beers in their hands.

"So did you have any more encounters with that woman, Davina?" Grace asked with a snicker.

Rosemary giggled loudly, remembering the next day at the Convention Center. "Oh yeah, did we ever. The next day, she looked like she was hurting so bad that I actually felt a little sorry for her."

But only a little.

"So, you crashed the erotic writer's convention dance party?" Grace began, leading her back to the subject they'd been discussing prior to Evan's exit.

Rosemary giggled gaily. "Yeah, we did. The dance was by invitation only, so I buzzed Tessa's cell phone from the hallway, and she and Max came out and got all three of us in."

"Lorelei DeVeaux is a man. I still can't believe it. So, did he and Tessa ride off into the moonlight?"

"When we finally left around two in the morning, they were really into each other on the dance floor, dirty dancing and grinding together. I danced with both Wes and Evan at the same time for a few dances. Let me tell you, that got some attention!"

"Let me guess! Everyone there thought you were cover models acting out one of your cover shoots from a ménage romance novel?"

"No, someone asked Max, and he told them we were the real deal! They all wanted to talk to us. But we promised Tessa and Lorelei the exclusive. They cannot wait to talk to *you*. So, is Rachel doing okay?"

"Oh yeah. She's healing up fast, and I wouldn't be a bit surprised if they're married by Christmas. Eli absolutely adores her. Don't you know they'd make gorgeous babies?"

Rosemary looked out the screen door and added, "Speaking of gorgeous babes, here come our men."

Chapter Sixteen

Mid-October…

Standing on the sunlit sidewalk outside of Cheaver's, Rosemary looked up into angry, brown eyes then turned and looked in to an equally irate pair of green eyes. She felt her core tighten, knowing she was *really* in for it this time, and probably not in a good way. Evan being angry didn't surprise her, under the circumstances. Wes *never* got angry. He wasn't wired that way. But looking in his eyes right now, she knew her ass was grass.

Rosemary held both palms up and implored almost silently before either of them could say a word. *"Not here, okay?"* Both men gritted their jaws, fuming. She didn't think it was her imagination when she felt heat spread across her ass cheeks. That realization made her face cheeks warm up to match.

Focusing on the issue at hand, she turned back to Randy as the Divine police officers handcuffed the thief she'd just chased down and apprehended with help from the store owner next door.

The thief had switched his worn boots for a pair of expensive new ones from their boot department and left the worn ones in the empty box then left the store without paying for them. Rosemary had watched the exchange from behind a two-way mirror in the stockroom. He'd carried a tool in his pocket, which he used to remove the theft deterrent device.

She'd followed the thief into the store next door, where she had alerted the store owner. The thief had been helping his mother and sister to hide merchandise from Arnold's store in the false bottom of a tote bag and a diaper bag. They'd confronted them moments before the police arrived. The officer searched them in the manager's office, he found all the merchandise they'd tried unsuccessfully to ditch on their way back, even the clothing folded and hidden beneath the tiny infant that lay sleeping in a stroller.

Rosemary had help in apprehending the thieves, but she'd still gone after a full-grown man alone because there had been no time to track Randy down and let him know. She would not have tried to apprehend the thief personally without the other store owner's help, but she knew none of that mattered right now. Her heart sank, and she felt confused.

Her safety was the issue, and the shoplifter's timing had really sucked. Wes and Evan had shown up while she was in the store next door, and one of her co-workers had informed them helpfully that Rosemary had just chased down a shoplifter and his thieving family. A bit of an exaggeration, she felt, but they didn't see the distinction between her merely following him and actually chasing him.

"Randy, I'm going to take lunch with Wes and Evan now. I'll finish the incident paperwork when I get back, okay?"

"Take extra time if you need it, sweetie." Randy pulled her aside and asked quietly, "Are your okay? You're looking pale all of a sudden."

"Maybe a little shook up, but I'll be fine," she replied, hoping like hell he didn't notice the way she was shaking.

"I know you feel it's your responsibility to protect the family store, sweetie, and I appreciate that you're so diligent. But it's not worth it if you get hurt in the process. I'd never forgive myself if something happened to you." Randy gently held her upper arms and looked into her eyes. She had to steel herself to keep the tears from falling at the concerned look she saw on his face. He smiled at her and said, "I'll see you in a bit."

Turning to Wes and Evan, she said, "I'll get my purse and be right out." Rosemary tried to smile at them but failed miserably. She could see the trouble brewing in their eyes.

They nodded and turned to each other, speaking quietly as she went to her office and retrieved her purse from her desk. She sat in her chair for a second to catch her breath.

Rosemary was certain they viewed this event as one of those times when she'd knowingly put herself in danger, but if she knowingly permitted thieves to get away with this sort of thing, Cheaver's would become an easy mark to other shoplifters. She couldn't let that happen and felt like this was one of her less enjoyable responsibilities. That probably wouldn't matter to Wes and Evan. It was best to get the confrontation over with. Maybe if she explained the situation to them, they'd understand.

Feeling a little calmer, Rosemary walked out of the stockroom and found her men talking with Randy while waiting for her at the front door. They were silent as they walked her out to Evan's pickup. They headed down FM 709 in the direction of their house.

Shit. "I thought we were going to Rudy's."

Wes sighed and looked down at her sitting between the two of them. "We need to go to the house instead. We can still go to Rudy's after we talk and deal with what happened today, if you want to. Or you can eat at the house if you'd like."

"Why do we have to go to the house?" she asked, already knowing the answer.

Wes sighed quietly. "You know why, baby. You shouldn't have been the one to chase down that thief. You could've been seriously injured or worse. You don't really understand how much you mean to us if you are willing to risk yourself that way." Evan pulled up to the house and shut off the ignition. He'd been silent the entire trip home. He climbed out of the truck and reached to help her down.

The men looked at her, and she realized she was trembling. She wasn't afraid of them spanking her. She was more afraid of them thinking she didn't care about their feelings. Rosemary didn't want them to think she didn't care if they were upset.

"I endangered myself, right? I know I did. I should've gotten someone else to come with me or called Randy from my cell phone. It wouldn't have gone as well if I hadn't had Arnold's help next door."

Sternly, Wes said, "*'Wouldn't have gone as well?'* You'd probably be in an ambulance right now, on your way to the ER." His normally tranquil green eyes were stormy with his emotions.

"Or worse," Evan added grimly as they escorted her up the front steps, and he unlocked the front door. Without preamble, they walked to her bedroom through the quiet house, and she followed behind.

"You're really going to…" Rosemary tried but failed to complete the sentence, in shock that they truly intended to *spank* her. On the one hand, she agreed with them that going after a thief twice her size was a *really* dumb thing to do. She should've had her cell phone on her. But sometimes you had to utilize the tools at hand to get the job done.

Evan looked almost sick and so disappointed. She realized she'd backed him, both of them, into a corner. "Yes, Rosemary. We talked about this, remember? I hope to hell this is the only time we ever have to do this. I hate the thought of spanking you for a reason other than your pleasure, but we made a promise to you. I warned you that, as far as you were able, you were to see to your own safety as a first priority. Today was an example of what *not* to do."

"But I had help. Arnold would not have let anything happen to me—"

"You are not Arnold's responsibility. What if that guy had been *armed*? What if he'd met up with other guys like him instead of two female family members and a baby?" Evan didn't paint a pretty picture.

"Well, that didn't happen, and I'm all right. It all ended well," she added weakly, knowing Wes and Evan were right.

"That doesn't matter. Come here," Evan said evenly as he sat on her big bed.

Rosemary walked over to him, not wanting to believe that he'd actually follow through on this.

"Do you remember your safe word?" His voice was soft and emotionless. She looked up at Wes, and he met her eyes, waiting expectantly. Something crumpled a little inside of her. Motionless, she looked back at Evan as he sat there patiently.

Part of her wanted to make a run for it, but she could see the conflict in his eyes. He didn't *want* to do this. Another part of her wanted to make this right with him. For them. She nodded, but didn't use the safe word.

"I need you to unbutton and remove your blue jeans, Rosemary."

"Why do I have to take off my jeans?" She didn't think she'd benefit from the additional humiliation of being undressed.

"Because I don't want to spank you too hard. I need to warm your bottom first so that you won't have any marks or be so sore. It needs to sting, but we don't want to physically harm you. Wes and I agree that you'll receive five licks." The muscles in his jaw were bunched and tense. She didn't want to push him any farther.

"I'm scared," she whispered, her fingers clutched together.

Wes knelt down in front of her, beside Evan, and took her hands. "Rosemary, please don't be scared. Our intent is not to harm you but to teach you to take care of yourself, to protect yourself. *Please*, can't we get this over with?" His tone implored, asking *her* for mercy. None of them wanted this, but they had to move forward.

Rosemary had waited years and had overcome all kinds of obstacles to be with these men. She knew they were right about apprehending the shoplifter. It was unsafe to follow him, regardless of the circumstances or her responsibilities. Rosemary came into this relationship with them knowing that they felt strongly about this issue. She also knew without a doubt that they'd never really hurt her. She trusted them.

Rosemary unbuckled her belt and unzipped the fly on her jeans. She toed her boots off and pushed her jeans down and slipped them off, pushing her socks off with them.

"Panties, too, baby," Wes said quietly, and she thought she heard a repressed groan slip from his throat.

Biting her lip uncertainly, she slid her black, lace thong off, confused that she felt a throb between her legs, whether at the thought of them seeing her naked or the thought that she was about to get a spanking, she wasn't sure. She wanted to kick herself. She had a feeling this *wasn't* going to be one of the fun spankings Evan had teased her about.

"Come here, baby." Wes led her to Evan's lap and drew her over his thighs as Evan laid a hand across her back to brace her. She was balanced on her tiptoes and fingertips. Wes stroked her arms, and she was grateful he stayed nearby, grounding her.

She whimpered when she felt Evan's other hand slide down her lower back and then over the cheeks of her ass. This was such a vulnerable position to be in, and her cheeks burned in mortification as she made close eye contact with Wes and saw that he hated this, too. Rosemary hung her head in shame when she almost opened her lips to appeal to Wes to save her from this spanking. She knew she could no longer play the brothers against each other like that. She needed to take her licks and get on with it.

Evan's callused hand massaged the cheeks of her ass firmly, and she felt warmth spread over her flesh. She cringed, knowing he could see her pussy in the position she was in and might even be able to tell that she was wet, insane as that thought was. His fingers and palms were thorough and firm, stroking and massaging her. A light pop landed on one cheek. It didn't even really sting.

Oh. This she could handle.

Another and another followed in quick succession. Deeper heat spread over the flesh of her ass. She imagined it was probably turning a nice pink color, and she felt confident that they'd be satisfied with having gone through the motions of spanking her. This wasn't bad at all.

Several more pops landed on her tingling skin, and she felt certain that he had already reached his allotment of five licks. Fine. At this rate, she'd give him an extra few freebies. Maybe even thank him afterward. Shoot, who needed a safe word for this?

She was *really* damp now, the blood coursed hotly through her cunt, making her clit more sensitive to each impact from his hand. She "got" the turn-on for erotic spankings now. At one point, she had to stifle a moan as the impact of his hand vibrated through her clit.

Rosemary thought she heard quiet communication of some sort between the men, and Wes said, "Count, baby."

She looked up, her curly black hair hanging in her eyes. "Huh?" She had to concentrate to understand him through her erotic buzz.

"Count each lick, now," Wes repeated.

"Huh?"

Smack! Wildfire lit up her ass.

In shock, she howled furiously. "Ow! Mother*fucker*!"

"Count," Evan ground out. "And watch your language. You're a lady."

"One, you son of a bitch! That *hurt*!" she screeched, writhing on his lap.

Smack! Harder than the first one, it stung harshly on her other ass cheek.

"Two! I'm going to get even for this!"

Smack! The loud crack of sound echoed around the room.

"Three! You're both going to *hell*!" she said, trying in vain to get away from Evan, but he easily held her immobile.

Smack! Her ass felt like it was on fire. She howled and hated the hitching sob that caught in her throat.

"Four. I hate you *both*! I said you were right. I won't do it again!" she screeched again, anticipating the fifth and hopefully final pop. A great sob welled from her.

When it finally landed, her voice broke, "Five." She lay still, waiting for them to release her. Evan's rough palm smoothed down her spine and over her derriere in soothing strokes. Unfortunately, his touch was having the opposite effect on her.

Rosemary heard Evan's shaky sigh as she caught her breath. Both her face and her ass felt like they were on fire. His hand sweeping over her ass seemed to intensify the heat emanating from her abused flesh. "I hope we never have to spank you like that ever again." He continued massaging her cheeks gently.

"Me neither," she whispered then gasped when his fingers strayed to the outer lips of her pussy and found her slick moisture there.

Evan groaned. "Rosemary, you're so wet." His fingers swirled through her wetness, caressing and teasing her. Wes's hand strayed over her derriere to join Evan's.

"Boomerang," she said with a whimper. They complied immediately and steadied her as she wobbled on her feet. She looked into their vulnerable eyes. They seemed confused that she'd used her safe word. "I might have enjoyed what you were doing at first, but *who wouldn't?* I always respond when you touch me. But then you spanked me for *real*," she whispered, rubbing her stinging ass. "You're going to have to give me a little time here. You can't go from punishing me to making love to me. It's too confusing." Tears tracked down her cheeks as she gathered her clothes.

Both men watched her, seeming unsure what to do next.

"Take me back to the store. I have work to do, and I need some time alone."

Evan's eyes beseeched her. "We need to talk, Rosemary. Please."

Her hand sliced through the air decisively, stopping him from saying more. "No. You've proved to me that you don't back down from a promise." When they would've said more, she silenced them with a look. "I need some time to myself. Please, Evan, Wes, just—don't."

Miserably, they watched her as she dressed quickly. Hitching sobs rasped from her chest every so often before she rushed from her bedroom and out the front door.

* * * *

Rosemary slipped her ringing phone from her purse and glanced at the screen as she ran through the stockroom doors and made a beeline for her office. That was Grace calling, and she needed privacy before she broke down in front of everybody.

"Hello."

"Hello? Rosemary? Are you okay?" Grace sounded concerned. Rosemary sat down at her desk in the back office after locking the door. She wasn't sure if the sound that came from her was a sigh or a sob, or maybe a combination. Her ass tingled as she settled slowly in her chair.

"Um, why?" Was Grace a member of the psychic network?

"Because Wes and Evan just showed up a minute ago, looking for Jack, Adam, and Ethan, and they look like someone ran over their brand-new puppy."

That news did elicit a sob from Rosemary. "They did?" She broke down, bawling like a big baby.

She'd managed somehow to keep it together on the drive back to the store. She'd refused to talk about the spanking with them. Cruelly, she'd used the protective skill she'd learned from living with her father on them and tuned them out. Even so, she'd still heard the inner struggle and love in their voices.

Rosemary was heartbroken, angry, and embarrassed all at the same time. She was a grown woman, and she didn't need her ass spanked as if she were an errant child. She'd hated the punishment but was also ashamed of herself for enjoying what had led up to it.

"I'll be right there. You stay put, okay?"

"'Kay." Rosemary ended the call and grabbed the box of tissue off her desk. She felt torn up inside. She was disappointed in herself for not doing as they'd asked. By placing herself in harm's way she'd put them in a difficult position, as well.

It confused Rosemary when moments after delivering the last painful swat, Evan and Wes's fingers had strayed to her wet, vulnerable pussy, finding for themselves the evidence of her earlier arousal. She'd been embarrassed that it had been there because aroused was the *last* thing she was by the time Evan was done.

She'd felt overwhelmed by the desire to be away from that room, away from that house, and away from them. Now, with all her heart, all she wanted to do was go back and have a do-over.

Shit, do over the whole damn day.

Rosemary would've put her cell phone in her pocket before she put her purse in her desk. She would've told someone to get Randy before she left the store. She'd have called 911 after locating the criminal and his family in the store, instead of confronting him with Arnold.

A spanking wouldn't have been necessary. It would've still been only a playful, erotic threat. With all her melodrama, she'd messed that up. They'd risked everything with her today to show her that she mattered to them, and she'd run from them. Like a child. A woman would've faced the situation head on.

Grace arrived five minutes later, and Rosemary told her everything.

Chapter Seventeen

Evan came in the back door with Wes, feeling exhausted and miserable. After finding and talking at length with Jack Warner, Ethan Grant, and Adam Davis, they'd returned to the house and spent the rest of the day hard at work in the shop, prepping to fill the orders that had come in, thanks to the Home Builder's Association convention.

Several of the online orders had contained special comments from customers regarding their charming and lovely sales representative. Instead of making him feel better, it'd only made Evan feel worse.

After snagging ice-cold beers from the kitchen, they both made their way back to the bathroom they shared. Bringing their beers into the shower with them, they left them sweating on a high shelf while they availed themselves of the multiple showerheads.

"I feel like utter dogshit," Evan muttered as he scrubbed his head mercilessly under the hot spray.

"Me, too."

Fucking doubtful. Evan was the one to always fuck things up between them.

Dejected, Evan continued, "I haven't felt this rotten since before Rosemary took us back. God, what did I do?"

"It's who you are, Evan. It's part of what makes you, you. It's also part of why she loves you. You like to be in control. She's not used to someone else calling the shots on her yet. But don't take on too much of the guilt because the three of us should bear it equally."

Bullshit. I could've kept my mouth shut. I could've let you take the lead. We wouldn't be in this mess now if I had.

"I shouldn't have done it. We could've had a heart-to-heart talk with her and left it at that."

Wes shrugged as he lathered. "Can't change the past. We'll give her a day or two to cool off. Maybe she'll talk to us then. Look at it this way. She knows now that we're serious about her not doing stupid things that endanger her anymore." Wes turned and started rinsing and looked Evan in the eye. "She was aroused by the warm-up. The spanking turned her off, and we got our wires crossed in the heat of the moment."

"I took too long preparing her."

Evan hit the valve and shut off the water. He dried off as Wes did the same, wrapping the towel around his hips. They exited the bathroom and went to their bedrooms. A flash of color caught Evan's eye as he looked behind his bedroom door for his robe. He glanced into Rosemary's bedroom, assuming she'd left something behind. Then he did a double take. He went in search of his brother and motioned him to follow him back down the hallway.

Her little, red cowgirl boots standing by her bed were what caught his eye, but Evan and Wes were both drawn by something else entirely. Rosemary lay curled on her side, cuddled to a pillow.

She was undressed and wearing Evan's thick fleece robe, which explained why he was unable to find it. She was sound asleep, her hair spread out in disarray around her. Evan could make out tracks on her cheeks where her tears had dried. She must've been really wiped out to not have heard them when they'd come in.

Evan whispered, "I'm such a *dick*. I spanked this little thing. What kind of fucking idiot am I?"

"An idiot completely in love with her. I'll leave you alone to talk to her," Wes murmured and then retreated from the room, pulling the door closed behind him.

In a quandary about what to do next, Evan stood there watching her for a minute, thinking over what Jack, Ethan, and Adam had told him. Sure he felt conflicted because he didn't *want* to be the one to initiate the reconciliation with her.

Ethan had put it into perspective for Evan. If he chose to be authoritarian about her safety, then it would *always* be him initiating the reconciliation until she understood how important this was to him.

Damn, he never wanted to go here again, had dreaded it from the moment they found out she'd gone off after a shoplifter. His little Rosemary, chasing a shoplifter almost twice her size. Evan didn't try to suppress his smile. Feisty little brat.

He knew it was a difficult position for her to be in, too. The store was a family business, and she felt like she needed to protect the store from assholes who thought their needs or wants came before those of the people who owned the establishments and the merchandise.

Evan sat down on the bed and caressed her cheek, erasing the tear stain. Her brows knit together in her sleep, and her breath hitched a little as if a sob were still trapped inside of her. It made him feel about two inches tall that she'd returned here to them and then cried herself to sleep.

Why wasn't she at her apartment pouting? Maybe she'd come here to work it out with them but hadn't quite been able to face them yet. The important thing to Evan was that she was *here*. Rosemary hadn't thrown in the towel. That brought another small smile to his face.

He fingered one of her long curls, rubbing the dark strands between his fingers. As far back as he could remember, her shiny, ebony curls had always fascinated him. He could recall even in kindergarten, reaching out to touch her hair, to run his fingers through the silky, dark curtain. Being surrounded by it when she bent over him to kiss him was particularly satisfying to him. He bent down to kiss the lock of hair then laid it aside, leaning over her to kiss her pale cheek.

Rosemary stirred, and then her eyes fluttered open. She looked at him, seeming a little disoriented at first. Turning onto her back, she gazed up at him with troubled eyes.

"Evan, I wish I could tell you I won't do stupid things in the future, but until I settle in, I may make more mistakes like this. Please don't give up on me."

He cratered a little when her lip trembled as she said the last words. "Rosemary, I should be the one worried about you giving up on me. I love you so much. Are you angry with me?"

Rosemary still seemed uneasy. "I'm more confused than anything else. When you were spanking my bottom lightly, I thought *that* was the punishment. The longer you went on, the more I enjoyed it. By the time you were done with the *real* punishment, I had accepted it and had given in to you. When you realized I was wet, it was humiliating to me, and I didn't want you to touch me at all. I needed time to recover and get dressed. I'm not a little doll you can play with on a whim like that."

Evan nodded, feeling ashamed. "I'm sorry I screwed with your head like that, Rosemary. You're absolutely right. We realized afterward how confusing it must've been for you. You know I'd never intentionally abuse you or want you to be afraid of me, don't you?"

Rosemary looked at him, and his heart contracted at the earnest love he saw reflected in her misty eyes. "Of course I know that, Evan. I know you risked a lot today, and I'm going to do my best to never need a real spanking from you again. Although," she added, her eyes twinkling as she gave him a little grin, "I did enjoy that first part quite a bit. You had my ass nice and warm, along with other parts, too."

She was torturing him. Evan smiled and leaned down to kiss her. "I know. I remember, naughty girl. I want to talk to you about something else for a minute."

Sitting up, Rosemary put a pillow behind her back. "What is it?"

"It's about Wes. He's put up with a lot over the years. It's in his personality to be a peacemaker, to handle difficult situations diplomatically. I noticed that you no longer go to him when you're upset with me, and I want you to know I appreciate that. He appreciates that, too, I imagine. I've always been more volatile, more prone to be jealous, and more likely to hog your time and energy. He's a giver, and I've always been a taker."

"Not necessarily, Evan. You give more than you realize."

"Thank you, but hear me out. When you want time alone with Wes, you don't need to make excuses to me or try to smooth it over with me. I loved our time alone in San Antonio. Well, except for the old ladies peeking in our keyhole. I could've done without all that, but I want you to feel free to spend time alone with him, too."

"I've been thinking about that a lot. I guess we're past the adjustment to being a threesome, and we need to move on to the 'three-equal-partners' phase, although it's hardly equal when one of the partners risks a *butt-whooping* when she steps out of line." Rosemary giggled as she turned on her hip and rubbed her ass. "My booty still tingles."

Evan rubbed her offended tush and said, "Well, maybe we'll have to do some delayed aftercare later. Would you like to stay the night?"

"Yes, but I'd like to spend it with Wes, like you suggested," she said, looking hopeful.

"It feels really weird to approve because I'll miss you, but that sounds like the right thing to do." His cock vehemently disagreed. But that's what cold showers and hand jobs were for.

"I brought my things for an overnight stay, just in case. Grace thought I should come and plan to stay until we had it all worked out between us."

"What would we do without her and those men?" Evan hated to even think about it. "We'd be lost, plain and simple." Still fumbling around, or worse.

Evan didn't tell Rosemary, but he'd talked to Grace earlier that afternoon also. When he'd seen her phone number on his caller ID, he'd been prepared to receive a silver-tongued brow beating. Evan was glad now that he'd answered her call. She hadn't said much of anything about the spanking one way or another. Grace had seemed more concerned about how he was feeling about it than whether or not it had happened.

Grace had also mentioned to Evan how much it helped when she spent time alone with Jack, Ethan, and Adam. It had strengthened their individual relationships, not divided them or put the other relationships out of balance. As a result, it made their whole family stronger. She'd made time to be alone with each of them from the beginning, which he and Wes had not done with Rosemary. Any time they'd gotten with her, up until this point, they had shared equally with her because her leisure time was a little scarce.

Rosemary's stomach grumbled loudly. Evan lifted her off the bed and held her in his arms. "Time to feed you, Rosemary. I'm sorry I made you cry."

"I forgive you, Evan. I love you." Rosemary hugged him tight, snuggling close to him. "I'm sorry, too."

Chapter Eighteen

Wes placed the lid over the skillet and wondered how the conversation was going in Rosemary's bedroom. He felt confident that Evan would work everything out with her because he knew Evan really loved her.

Most of her doubts about their relationship had been laid to rest, minus today's little blip on the radar. Not that he held that completely against Evan. She'd placed herself in a dangerous situation that could've had serious repercussions, so he'd agreed with his brother about what needed to happen. Rosemary had always had a reckless streak. Maybe that was because they'd always been there to save her. A wry smile came to his lips. He couldn't think of anyplace he'd rather be.

Hearing the door open down the hallway, Wes smiled. That hadn't taken long at all.

"Mmm, something smells yummy in here." Rosemary trotted into the kitchen and wrapped her arms around his neck when he bent down to her. He lifted her up, and she wrapped her legs around him as he nuzzled into her fragrant throat.

"Mmm, something smells yummy in here, too." Wes held her close and pressed his lips against her luscious neck. His cock agreed, judging by the way it stood up and took lascivious notice.

"I meant to *eat*, silly!" She giggled when he headed south to the cleavage revealed as Evan's robe slipped open and then nuzzled deeper, growling hungrily.

"So did *I*," Wes murmured as he looked up and met Evan's eyes over her shoulder. Evan had a relaxed grin on his face, and he used sign language to convey that he would be in his bedroom, allowing them some alone time before supper.

Feeling like a little kid let loose in a candy factory, Wes planted Rosemary on the marble countertop. Grasping the belt of the robe, Wes pulled it loose and pushed open the front of the robe as he parted her knees and stepped between them. No longer giggling, she watched him through half-lidded eyes as he drew her to the edge of the counter against him.

Rosemary wrapped her calves wrapped around his hips and slid her fingers into his hair. Unsnapping the front clasp of her black lace bra, he pushed it away so that he could hold her lush breasts in his hands and feast and suckle on them one at a time. His cock jumped at the first low moan from her. He buried his face in her satiny cleavage and held her plastered to him.

Her rasping sighs were like music to his ears, and his cock tingled with need at the sound. While he kissed her breasts, he held her around the waist with one arm, lifted her, and hooked the back waistband of her lacy panties with the other hand and pulled them off. He pulled away from her only long enough to get them over her knees and flung them away.

"You intoxicate me, Rosemary. I want you."

They were both panting as he pressed her to lie down on the empty countertop. Her cheeks were flushed, and her eyelids slid closed as he slid his hands up her thighs in a lingering caress, sliding over her hipbones and ribcage to her breasts again. She looked incredibly decadent and sexy, laid out for him like that, ready to be devoured. Her pussy glistened, and her lips parted as she squirmed under his light strokes. He longed to fit his cock to her cunt and plunge in with one solid stroke.

"Sometimes I feel like I've wanted you my whole life, Rosemary."

Wes pressed his lips to her bare, baby-soft mound, and she breathed out a high-pitched moan. From his vantage point, he could easily catch the scent of her arousal. He kissed his way down to her slit.

He brushed his lower lip against her pussy. "Part of me wanted to die when I couldn't have you, baby. It was worse than just waiting for you because I knew what it felt like to make love to you."

Rosemary panted ecstatically, and he kissed her lips and then slid his tongue into the slick flesh within her slit. The sweet tang of her juices was like ambrosia on his tongue. She trembled beneath him as he teased her clit, her hips surging against him in invitation as he petted her and slid his fingers around her entrance. He rested her thighs on his shoulders, and her heels pressed into his back, trying to draw him closer to her.

"I want to make up for all the nights we spent apart. I want to be inside you and never leave."

Rosemary didn't speak, but then again, she didn't need to. Her juices dripped from her pussy, and her trembling increased as he once again slid his tongue between her lips, tasting her and then sliding over her clit. He watched close up as he laved the reactive little bundle of nerves, flicking the tender little hood of flesh that covered it, loving the way she shuddered as her pussy quivered for him, visual evidence of her arousal, small though it was. His cock ached to feel her little pulses, too.

She inhaled deeply, and Wes knew she'd scream as he closed his lips around her clit and suckled, increasing the suction bit by bit until her moans turned into sobs then her sobs turned into screams as her orgasm broke all around her. Her fingers slid roughly through his hair, and she held the back of his head like she didn't want him to pull away from her yet.

Silly girl, he wasn't going anywhere.

He released her clit, allowing her to come down only slightly before he slid a finger into her entrance, and her back arched, and she moaned again. He slid another finger inside her and stroked her G-spot. He touched lightly at first, listening to her breathing and paying attention to the way she moved. When she was ready, he increased the pressure and began strumming her clit again with his thumb.

Rosemary moved her hips rhythmically against his hand, and he watched in fascination as she tensed, smiling angelically, and came for him again. Her upper body was flushed from her earlier orgasm, but her cheeks blushed a darker rose as her lips parted on a blissful moan. He applied more pressure to her clit and continued strumming her G-spot, knowing it was a matter of seconds before her third orgasm came. His dick pulsed with a hungry ache as he watched her. He had to consciously hold back his burning release.

She arched her back and went completely still. Her pussy flooded honey in his hand, and he knew that it had broken over her hard when, a split second later, she released an ear-piercing scream followed by several seconds of high-pitched sobs that were heart wrenching to listen to in their intense vulnerability. He licked up every satisfying drop of honeyed cream she gave him.

He promised himself hours of decadent revelry inside her later and didn't take her against the kitchen counter like the beast inside him wanted to. He'd save that for his bed and the quiet solitude of his room.

Trying to catch her breath, Rosemary held onto him and lay quietly. Wes released her thighs after he was done and gently lifted her noodle-limp body, holding her against his chest. Her eyes were dazed as she looked at him, sighed dreamily, and cuddled to him.

Softly, she said, "I hope dinner's not burned."

"I turned it down low before you came in here. Are you hungry?"

Rosemary chuckled, "Maybe in a few minutes. Right now sensation is all centered below the waist and it's all goo-ood."

"Damn, I'll say. Better than good."

She reached inside her robe and laughed as he appreciatively watched her jiggle her generous breasts back into her bra. "What? Gotta get the girls nice and even."

Helping to close her robe and tie the belt, Wes lifted Rosemary down from the counter and held her to him, whispering and stroking her back and hair. He didn't release her until her legs no longer wobbled under her.

"Where did my panties get to?"

"I don't know. I'm sure they're around here somewhere."

"I'll go get dressed."

He pulled her to him again before she left the kitchen and kissed her then whispered, "I want you tonight, Rosemary. *That* was just an appetizer."

* * * *

Wes had no doubt that Evan had heard Rosemary's screams earlier. Both he and Evan loved that she didn't hide her pleasure from them, and he looked forward to round two later that evening. True to his word, Evan retreated to his bedroom to watch a movie after they shared the evening meal.

Wes found her in her bathtub, up to her chin in scented bubbles. Rosemary's eyes twinkled as she murmured invitingly, "Join me?"

"You don't have to ask me twice."

"But I must warn you, my bubbles may make you girly-scented." She giggled playfully as she ogled him while he stripped.

"I think my masculinity can withstand your 'girly-scented' assault just fine. Come here." He joined her in the tub and sat on the contoured seat with the whirlpool jets pointed at his lower back. His cock reared up as soon as she settled her curvy fanny across his thighs.

"How is your bottom feeling this evening? Any pain or marks? Stand up for a second."

She complied and said, "It's still tender when I sit on it but not painful." She wiggled her ass at him after he'd made sure there were no marks left behind.

"Good. That's why we warm it up before a spanking. So that it won't be as sore, and so you won't have marks. We don't want that." He hummed in admiration at her enticing little wiggle, grasped her hips, and held her still while he licked, nipped, and kissed her ass cheeks. "We adore this little ass so much, baby."

"Hmph. There's nothing *little* about my ass." She giggled as he pulled her back down onto his lap, one hand grasping and squeezing each cheek.

"It's two perfect handfuls. Ask Evan and he'll tell you exactly the same thing. We love it bobbing and swaying when you walk away, we love it wiggling when you dance, and *mmm*, we love to hold on to it when we're making love to you. It's perfect."

"Thank you." She sloshed around and turned in his lap so she was straddling his hips, facing him. He massaged her ass and leaned back against the sloped side of the tub, enjoying the feel of her as she settled against his chest, fitted perfectly with him.

Playing with a curl that had come loose from her clip, he asked, "Is there a reason we haven't eloped yet? I know you aren't afraid of commitment, but is there something that still has you unsure about us?" His palms traced up and down her ribs.

Rosemary shook her head. "No, not now. I wanted to wait until after the Christmas season, that's all. The end of January or beginning of February would be a great time. Grand Cayman should be perfect then. I'm also going to cut my hours and delegate some of my responsibilities to others. I talked to Randy about it before I came over this afternoon."

Wes knew this was a big deal to her, though she spoke of it nonchalantly.

"We don't expect you to quit your job. That's your family's store. We know it's important to you."

"The store has been my life for too long. Randy understood, and right after the holidays, we'll start making adjustments. I'll still be there in my usual capacity during November and December, but I won't take on extra hours."

"You're sure this is what you want?" The last thing he wanted was for her to feel like she had to make a choice between them and the store.

"Yeah. I need more time with the two of you than my hours allow right now. Before, the store was my home, so I didn't mind. Now, you and Evan are my home."

The idea that she wanted to spend more time with them pleased Wes greatly, and he knew Evan would feel the same.

"I'm relieved that the timing with the Thanksgiving and Christmas holidays is the only issue."

"It really is. Actually, I've been thinking that I might go ahead and move over here. I'd need to—"

"I'll go get boxes *right now*," Wes said enthusiastically. "We have two trucks, and we can have you moved in one day. Say the word, baby. We're so ready for you to be with us. Just say when."

Rosemary threw her arms around him and hugged him hard. "Good. My deposit will pay the penalty for breaking the lease early. You can move me this weekend if you have time."

"We'll *make* time. Hot damn, wait until Evan finds out."

"Wait until the girls find out!"

"We're going to love having you over here, permanently," Wes murmured, his mood shifting as he drew her to him and kissed her. His lips brushed hers, and she tilted into his kiss, teasing his lower lip with the tip of her tongue. He plundered her mouth, sealing his lips to hers, his tongue dueling with hers in a teasing game of give and take until she was breathless. His cock was hard against her mound, and she grasped it gently, causing him to shudder in pleasure.

"Are you done with your soak, baby, because I'm ready to make love to you right now." His cock was throbbing to be inside her. He had to still her hand from moving on his cock because he wanted to come so badly.

Rosemary stood in the tub, and he smiled up at her as the hot water cascaded down her body. Using a wash cloth, she rinsed all the bubbles off, keeping her eyes on him as she did this, smiling at his obvious enjoyment. A seductive smile lit her face as he rose from the water, and she could see how big and hard he'd gotten while watching her. No question about it, his cock wanted to go *home*, right *now*.

Still smiling, the little minx turned her back to him and leaned over a little, grasping the side of the tub, making sure he got a nice, long glimpse of her pussy as she climbed carefully from the slippery tub onto the mat and toweled off. He opened the drain and followed her out. She hung up her towel and meandered out to her bedroom, taking her time while he watched her swaying ass hungrily. Finally, he'd had enough, and he snuck up behind her and lifted her squealing in his arms and tossed her on the bed.

He crawled over her like a jungle cat about to pounce, and she asked, "Did you light candles?"

"I don't want to make love to you in the dark. I want to see you while I fuck you."

She stretched both arms over her head and rested them above her, sliding her fingers seductively into her hair. "Me, too."

He glanced over at their reflection in the free-standing, full-length mirror that had been repositioned beside her dresser. "That's also been arranged."

She smiled at his reflection in the mirror and then looked at him. "Clever man, to plan ahead so thoroughly."

"I'm glad you had a nap this afternoon because we're going to lose some sleep tonight."

Wes made love to Rosemary that night with a slow, burning intensity that he felt sure would send him to the borderlands of insanity. He drove her over the edge three times, using his tongue, his fingers, and even the tip of his nose before he ever even let her see his cock. He took her orally, vaginally, and in a final, overwhelming crescendo, he took her anally because she begged him to while he teased her with a vibrating dildo. That time, when she came she couldn't hold back the howling scream that erupted from her throat.

He wasn't satisfied until she'd come six times, and then he'd poured his burning release into her ass as her pussy spasmed on the dildo with climax number seven. By the time he was finished, her limbs were the equivalent of overcooked spaghetti. After he cleaned and tucked her in, he'd taken a quick shower himself then rejoined her in the bed.

Amazingly, Rosemary was still awake, and once he settled beside her, she snuggled to him, scooching as close as she could. Finally, he chuckled and pulled her on top of him. She sighed happily and tucked her head under his chin. They talked until late into the night, whispering and laughing, making plans and sharing their dreams.

As they talked, Wes stroked her all over, the way he'd dreamed of doing on thousands of lonely nights in the past. It was as if his hands were starving to touch her and he couldn't get enough. This time together had been long overdue.

"Are you comfortable like this, Rosemary?" Wes asked as he kneaded her derriere.

She snuggled closer and replied, "Of course, why? Are you comfortable?"

"God, yes. Stay where you are all night. I want you all over me."

Rosemary's breath puffed over his chest hair, and she wiggled against him. "Something tells me that parts of you would like to do more than just have me all *over* you," she said, arching and flexing her hips over the erection growing against her abdomen. He'd wondered if she'd noticed yet.

It's the feel of your skin under my hands. I can't get enough, and I guess my cock agrees."

Chapter Nineteen

Rosemary felt even closer to Wes after talking for so long with him. She was amazed she hadn't conked out, but it was as if she were hungry for this time with him, wanting to catch up with him.

His hands had never stopped their languid stroking the whole time they talked, and she felt like he was memorizing every inch of her. She could honestly say that this was the tenderest, most vulnerable moment they'd ever shared together since all those years ago when he'd taken her virginity and lost his own in the process.

Rosemary had noticed immediately when his cock had hardened, unsurprised when her weeping slit had eagerly responded.

Rising over him, she slid her slick pussy back and forth a few delicious, grinding times then slid forward and arched her back, allowing him to penetrate her. She lay back down on his torso, tucking her head under his chin and moved over him in slow, unhurried waves.

"Ride me, baby." His hands grasped her hips, and he helped her move in the way he liked. He loved it, judging by his moans and whispered encouragement, and he released her hips as she set her own pace. She rode him in smooth, sinuous strokes.

"Fuck, that feels unbelievable, but I want you to stop for a second."

After climbing off, she allowed him to turn her toward the mirror on her hands and knees. She'd watched him earlier, too, as he'd slid his cock into her pussy with her knees pushed back practically to her ears, and when he'd taken her ass from behind as he'd slowly slid his cock into her tight hole.

"Watch me."

He retrieved the small fingertip vibrator from her bedside table drawer, and she felt her pussy contract for him, begging to get the show on the road. She looked into his eyes in the mirror.

He traced fingers over her swollen lips, and then she felt his broad head at her opening. Rosemary moaned in bliss and kept her eyes locked on his face as she felt him slide in to the hilt. He didn't try to hide what he was feeling in an effort to appear macho or strong. He pleasured them both, pumping in slow, thorough strokes.

He'd slid the fingertip vibrator on at some point and then smoothed his hand down her abdomen and over her mound. She clenched around him in anticipation of the pleasure to come.

His vibrating fingertip made contact with her clit, the sensation quickly driving her to the brink as he stroked her in ever smaller circles. She looked into Wes's eyes, moaning hoarsely as he brought her to orgasm. Dropping the vibrator from his hand, he clutched her hips and pounded firmly into her.

He looked majestic behind her, grasping her strongly, the one in control. His handsome face was a play of emotions—ecstasy, domination, and finally satisfaction as his body tensed, his teeth gritted together in a grimace. He growled his pleasure deeply as he held her to him, his seed pulsing forth into her spasming pussy.

He bowed his head, and his hands slid all over her. Wrapping his arms around her, Wes lifted her to rest against his chest. He slid a hand across her pelvis, his fingers resting across her mound and the top of her thigh, the other arm wrapped around her torso. He nuzzled her throat as she tilted her head back to rest against his shoulder.

"Look," he whispered lovingly, gazing at her in the mirror, draped against him, his cock still buried between her widespread thighs. "That is the most beautiful thing I've ever seen."

His cock still pulsed inside her, a mark of possession that she welcomed with her whole heart.

"It is beautiful, Wes. I'll never forget this moment."

Rosemary had pondered how she would feel after the opportunities to spend time alone with her men presented themselves. Would there be hints of jealousy between Wes and Evan? The question always refrained in her mind over whether their relationship would swing out of balance.

Having close male friends involved in an even more complicated arrangement seemed to give them a healthy foundation because she'd never sensed the fomenting of jealousy between them.

Evan had retreated to his room as the evening progressed, after kissing her goodnight. He'd been pretty specific in encouraging her to spend the night alone with Wes. A satisfying sense of relief filled her because she knew he did it to decrease her worry. Evan must've known if there was even a hint that he'd retreated to his room less than willingly, that she would've worried about it the whole time. Which would've ruined her time with Wes. Now she could focus on pleasing Wes and receiving pleasure from him without holding back.

Wes's lips slid with intoxicating effectiveness from her throat to the flesh behind her ear. "Evan loves you so much. He only wants your happiness."

She chuckled and smiled at him, a lump forming in her throat at the love reflected in his eyes.

"Wow, now you're reading my mind," she whispered.

Her breath shuddered from her as his hand caressed from her mound over her abdomen, to cup one of her breasts. She loved the way his work-roughened hands felt on her skin. Whenever either of them held her, she felt safe.

She watched unabashedly as he slid his other hand from her shoulder to hold the other breast in that hand. It was undeniably erotic, watching the way he touched her, the way her breasts slightly overfilled his hands as he cupped them tenderly. Her pussy quivered reflexively when he rubbed his thumbs over her peaked nipples, causing him to growl at the sensation.

Rosemary looked into his eyes then and squeezed him with her pussy muscles while simultaneously grinding her buttocks back against him. She smiled when the movement against him shifted his cock slightly inside of her, and she sensed that he was still hard.

Holding her to him, he slid two fingers to her slit. Rosemary gasped as he found her clit and slowly stroked her. Listening to the wet sound of his fingers sliding through her well-lubricated flesh lit her up faster than she would've believed possible. Feeling what he was doing while simultaneously watching and listening to it was explosively erotic.

Then he spoke as he thrust gently against her. "I love this beautiful pussy. Can you feel what you do to me? I'm hard again, just from looking and touching when I should be comatose right now," he whispered, chuckling. "If I could ask to stay somewhere forever, it would be inside you like this."

He thrust inside her as she continued to grind against him, his fingers swirling around her clit until she was gasping.

Their lovemaking didn't follow the previous slow rise to tumultuous, heated, blinding ecstasy. This fire inside them burned low, their movements staying slow but searingly intense against each other.

It was as if they were locked in that unhurried, grinding dance until they were ready to combust, their eyes locked on each other. She neared the crest of her orgasm, and instead of her movements becoming more pronounced, more physical, her body moved less sinuously, her muscles locking down within her, clamping hard as a vise on the cock strumming her body to screaming crescendo.

"Yes," he murmured as he slid from her depths and thrust deep and slow, strumming her G-spot firmly as he held her. Her head fell back, her lips wide open, her back arching hard as she moaned in bliss.

Melting against him, she allowed him to hold her up, her hands still clutching his shoulders with ineffectual strength. She couldn't even feel her hands, much less know how she was able to hold on to him. Her body was covered in a sheen of sweat, and it sent a shiver down her torso when she felt Wes's tongue flick out to lick her shoulder.

"We can build a huge house and fill it with the finest furniture our hands can create, but this, right here, is home for me," he murmured as he kissed the place his tongue had been. "I'm so glad you never gave up, baby."

"I've loved you and Evan since you were little boys. Giving up on you two was never an option."

Epilogue

The following weekend...

"Okay, sweet cheeks. That's the last of the boxes," Luke Garner, Wes and Evan's father, said to Rosemary as the men came in the door that led out into the garage.

Between her and Mary, Wes and Evan's mom, she'd managed to get all of her clothing and personal items unpacked and put away.

There was furniture and other stuff stored in the garage that she would have to sort through, but she was out of her apartment completely and moved in with her men.

She and Mary had finished opening all the foil-wrapped containers from Rudy's, which they had just returned with moments before.

Rosemary trotted over to Luke and gave him a big hug. "Thank you so much for helping me move in. It means a lot to me. Not everybody's parents would approve of me moving in with Wes and Evan before the wedding."

Mr. Garner hugged her back and patted her shoulder with his big, callused hand. "Rosemary, not everybody has watched you all grow up together and love each other the way we have. I'll confess I don't fully get the dynamic that you three live with, but I do know love when I see it. You love my sons well enough for two women, and they adore you. I don't care what anybody else thinks."

Rosemary hugged him again, a little teary-eyed when he kissed the top of her head. Luke and Mary Garner were two of a kind.

"That's right, honey. You already know that's how I feel, too." Mary said as she got on her hands and knees, sifting through a bottom cabinet.

Somehow, word had gotten out around town that Rosemary was engaged to and moving in with both Wes and Evan Garner. Some people assumed she was engaged to Wes and moving in with him and that Evan was their roommate, but many others knew the truth of it. That she was in love and living with both of them, preparing to marry Wes.

Rosemary had an ugly confrontation with Elizabeth Owens and one of her self-righteous friends in Stigall's a few days before when she'd been shopping with Mary for gifts for Wes and Evan's birthdays, which were both at the beginning of December. *Mary* had promptly told Elizabeth off and asked her to mind her own damned business.

Her voice muffled inside a bottom cabinet, Mary said, "Rosemary, *please* tell me that you're going to finally organize this kitchen." She grunted as she backed out of a cabinet filled with pots and pans, with a package of paper napkins in her hand. "Those boys have got their workshop organized like a master chef's gourmet kitchen, but this beautiful, marble-countered, hand-crafted masterpiece is stocked like a bunch of *frat* boys live in it!"

Rosemary giggled and said, "It's horrendous, isn't it? And yes, it's at the top of my list. Next time you come over, it will be all organized. I hope you're all hungry."

"So have you decided on a date?" Mary asked as she passed the large foil pan filled with meat around the dining table.

Wes replied, "Rosemary is still up in the air about what to do with her parents, but we've decided on the first weekend in February. There's a beach resort on Grand Cayman that we liked the looks of, and they sound like they specialize in throwing beach weddings. They have rooms still available for that weekend, and there are several other resorts and hotels that are close by."

"Yes," Rosemary said, "the beach is beautiful, and they have an overlook that is perfect for the reception afterward. I haven't said anything to my parents though, beyond telling them that I'm engaged, though."

Mary and Luke smiled at her, seeming to understand her dilemma. They'd watched helplessly as her parent's endless dramas played out over the years, heedless of the damaging effect it'd had on Rosemary as she grew up.

Over the years, Rosemary had come to think of herself as their adopted daughter, and they'd given her the stability she'd needed whenever they could. She supposed that was one of the reasons Mary and Luke were unsurprised when they had told them of their plans for a life together.

Mary said, "They aren't the first divorced couple who had to cope with attending the wedding of their grown child. Do you want to know what I'd suggest?"

"Of course, Mary."

"Tell them what your plans are. Let them decide on their own, whether they want to come. Expect them to act like adults and don't worry about whether or not they get along. We already decided that we're going to be there, didn't we Luke?" Mary asked as Luke placed a gentle hand over hers.

"Yep. We're going to come to the wedding, and then after the reception, your mom and I are going to fly over to Little Cayman to another resort there and stay for a few days and have a second honeymoon," Luke said, smiling at Mary, his eyes a little dazed. Mary blushed when he leaned toward her and gave her a tender kiss.

Wes, Evan, and Rosemary grinned at each other. Wes rolled his eyes and chuckled while Mary and Luke were lost in the moment. Then Rosemary noticed Wes squint when he looked toward the ceiling.

Wes glanced at Evan and her and then over at his parents quickly. Evan looked back at him silently, his eyebrows joining together in a questioning look before looking up toward the ceiling. Rosemary watched the two of them in the brief non-verbal communication that lasted only milliseconds before looking up to see what had drawn their eyes.

The first thing to catch her eye was the wrought iron and blown glass light fixture over the table. She looked more closely and saw what it was that threw the symmetry of the light fixture off slightly. There was a black lace thong hung on the gathered center of the unit.

Rosemary looked back down at her plate, clamping her lips together, and then glanced up at Wes. He was exchanging a look with her and Evan before he slid his hand over his face, trying to hide a smile.

"Oh, sorry, guys. That was probably more mush than you wanted to see, huh?" Mary asked with a giggle as she looked over at them, thankfully misinterpreting their blushing faces and embarrassment.

Rosemary giggled, able to respond first, and replied, "I hope we're half as romantic as you are after thirty-eight years of marriage, Mary. Don't you dare apologize for being in love."

After dinner, Mary and Rosemary cleared the table while the men retired to the back deck to light the fire pit and enjoy the crisp fall evening.

Mary stood beside her, pouring wine into two glasses for them, and said, "I was hoping that you might be willing to help me do a little online shopping sometime. Maybe direct me to some good Web sites? I wanted to get some things for our trip to the wedding and Little Cayman."

"Sure. The weather will be warm and breezy down there. Did you want to look for a bathing suit or casual wear?"

"Well, yeah. But I was hoping…maybe you would help me find some *other* things?" Mary said, giggling.

"*Oh?*" Rosemary asked knowingly. "What kinds of *other* things?"

"I was thinking some *really* sexy lingerie?"

"Yeah? I can definitely point you in the right direction," Rosemary said with a snicker, lifting her glass of wine to her lips as she flipped the light switch in the kitchen off. "What did you have in mind?"

Mary giggled as they passed through the kitchen on the way to the back door, glancing up at the light fixture. "Oh, I was thinking something in black lace would be perfect."

The two of them howled with laughter as they went out the door together.

THE END

WWW.HEATHERRAINIER.COM

ABOUT THE AUTHOR

Heather Rainier lives and writes in South Central Texas. Her stories offer up the content of her fantasies, with autobiographical humor, triumph and tragedy mixed in.

Heather believes that life doesn't always present love to us in neat little sanitized packages. Sometimes we have to seize the day, live life with no regrets, forget the past, never give up, learn to trust, and dare to live, even in outrageous circumstances.

When not happily typing at her keyboard, Heather is usually busy corralling her kids, volunteering at local schools, or loving on her smokin' hot husband, who thankfully loves to cook.

Also by Heather Rainier

Ménage Everlasting: Divine Creek Ranch 1: *Divine Grace*
Everlasting Classic: Divine Creek Ranch 2: *Her Gentle Giant, Part 1: No Regrets*
Everlasting Classic: Divine Creek Ranch 2: *Her Gentle Giant, Part 2: Remember to Dance*
Ménage Everlasting: Divine Creek Ranch 3: *Heavenly Angel*
Everlasting Classic: Divine Creek Ranch 5: *Spurs and Heels*

Available at
BOOKSTRAND.COM

Siren Publishing, Inc.
www.SirenPublishing.com

CPSIA information can be obtained at www.ICGtesting.com
225510LV00006B/109/P

9 781610 345026